BOOKS BY SUPRIYA KELKAR

Ahimsa

Supriya Kelkar

Strong as Fire, Fierce as Flame

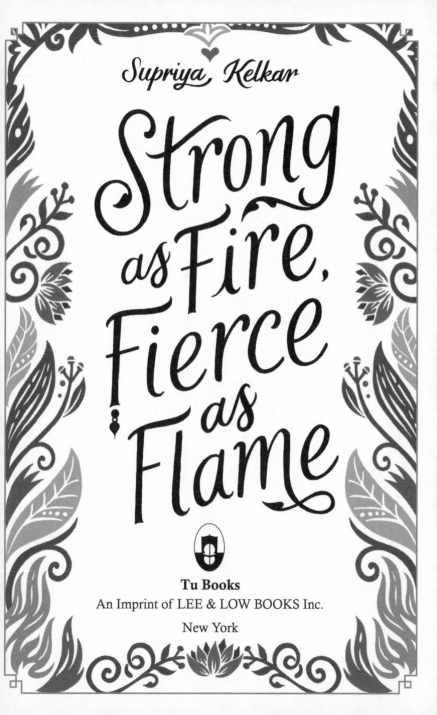

Tu Books

An Imprint of LEE & LOW BOOKS Inc.

New York

TU BOOKS, an imprint of LEE & LOW BOOKS Inc.,
95 Madison Avenue,
New York, NY 10016
leeandlow.com

Manufactured in the United States of America

Printed on paper from responsible sources

Edited by Stacy Whitman
Book design by Sheila Smallwood
Typesetting by ElfElm Publishing
Book production by The Kids at Our House
The text is set in Calisto MT and Madali
Interior illustrations by Kate Forrester
Map art by Vikki Zhang
10 9 8 7 6 5 4 3 2 1
First Edition

Cataloging-in-Publication Data is on file with the Library of Congress

To Aaji, Bhausaheb, Bapu, Vahini,
Anand Ajoba, and Nalu Aaji

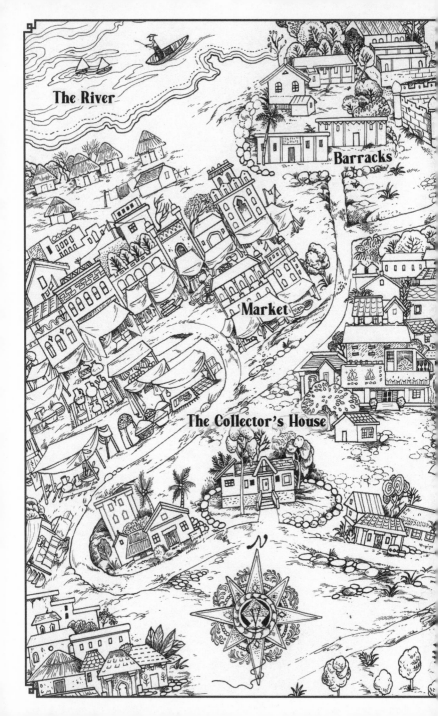

The Town of Indranagar

The Magazine

The Bungalow on the Hill

Meera's Quarters

The Keenes' Bungalow

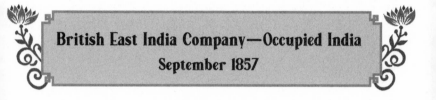

British East India Company—Occupied India
September 1857

Chapter 1

My father taught the village boys right outside our little earthen home, but I wasn't a boy, so I didn't get to learn. That didn't stop me from trying, though. I sat high up in the tree at the end of our front yard, peering through the rubbery green leaves as my father started the school day like he always did: by writing the date on the black writing slate in his hand.

The boys, sitting cross-legged on the ground, copied the date on their slates. Although I couldn't read what was written, I knew what the day was before Babuji said it. Because in three days it was my thirteenth birthday, and my mother had been talking about it for weeks.

"Meera!" Ma called out to me as she rushed from the doorway of our tiny rectangular home, a wicker bowl in her hand. The handful of distracted village boys turned her way, and Babuji gave her a sharp look for disturbing his class. Ma quickly grabbed the pleats of her dusty indigo sari as she hurried apologetically past my father toward me.

"Meera," she whispered, swatting at my dangling left foot until I was forced to jump down, "you know you aren't allowed in his class. We have to get to the market." The vermilion bindi crumpled in the sudden wrinkles between her eyebrows. "We only have three more days."

Ma bit her lip like she always did when she was sad and began down the village path, guiding me along. We passed house after house still glistening with dewdrops from the night before, bleating goats, and a prowling orange-and-white cat, its fur matted with dirt. And Ma kept chewing at her lower lip. She wasn't sad because I was turning thirteen in three days. She was sad because in three days, I was going to have to move in with my husband and his family. I was sad too. And frustrated that I didn't have a say in any of this. After all, it was my life, my future, that was being determined for me.

Krishna and I were married when we were little. Ma loved to tell the story, far out of Babuji's earshot, of what happened when I saw the sacred fire that we would circle in the ceremony. I got so nervous at seeing the flames up close, at feeling the heat against my tiny sari, I'd had an accident. In Babuji's lap. I bet not many brides wet themselves on their wedding day. But what did you expect from a scared four-year-old?

"You'll remember to behave yourself there, won't you, Meera?" Ma asked as we walked past the large round stepwell you could gather water from or swim inside. We turned toward the tiny gray stone temple that peacocks pranced around. I gazed at the birds, at the brilliantly colored male who got all the attention from passersby for his stunning display of feathers while the peahens seemed to do all the work, caring for their young in the background.

"And you'll listen, right? You won't stare off at the birds when Krishna's mother tells you to do something?"

Taking in the winking golden eyes on the peacock's feathers, I shook my head. "No birds. I'll do whatever she says," I replied like the obedient daughter I was supposed to be, despite how unfair I thought it all was.

Ma held me tighter as we passed a couple women sitting on the ground outside the temple, dressed in white cotton saris with shaved heads and hands out. They sang songs to beg for money. They were widows who often came from tiny homes with large households that had too many mouths to feed. Sometimes, when they became a burden, some widows would be forced out of their homes. With nowhere to go, they often begged at our temple, wearing white because they weren't allowed to wear colors after their husbands died.

I scrunched the fabric of my orange-and-maroon sari as I looked at one of them. Her eyes were cloudy gray with age, her wrinkles set deep in sadness. It must not have felt nice to be kicked out of your house or not get to wear colors anymore, and maybe some felt jealous of the thousands of widows whose families didn't abandon them, whose children lovingly took care of them until they died of old age.

But being an abandoned widow sure seemed better than the other alternative: sati. Sati was a rare, ancient tradition that only a few families practiced, in which some widows, who didn't have young children to care for, sacrificed themselves on their husbands' funeral pyre to join them in the afterlife.

At the sight of the widows, a desperate flutter began in my belly. I hastened down the lane past them with Ma. The widows' songs soon faded to a faint whisper in the wind as we neared the market, full of stalls of fruits and vegetables, clay and metal vessels, and grains, all shaded by canopies of orange, red, and yellow fabrics on either side of the small, well-worn path. The voices of villagers bargaining and merchants announcing what they were selling filled the air as we entered the crowded bazaar.

"I polished the bangles today," Ma said, examining some grains of millet in a basket at a stall.

"Again? You've been cleaning them every day," I replied, fanning my face for a little break from the humid air.

"It's your dowry. I want it to be perfect." Ma moved to the next stall.

I nodded, following her. My dowry was the amount promised to Krishna's family for taking care of me when we got married. It was tradition, and my parents were giving away much of what they had in those two gold bangles that made up my dowry. I ran my fingers over some clay pots, thinking about how, thanks to dowries, some girls like me were a burden for their poor families, just like those temple widows were burdens for their families after they were married.

Ma stopped to purchase a tiny cup and handed it to me. "Take it with you to your new home and think of me every time you drink your water."

That sad quiver started in my gut again as I squeezed the cup against my chest, shadowing Ma farther into the market down the twisting lane cramped with people.

We dashed past a handful of men puffing on their beedis, holding our breath as they exhaled the sickening smoke, and turned past the house of the jaggery merchant. A dozen people were gathered outside it, laughing and clapping as they sang a folk song. Right in front of the house, an old lady dressed in a gold-and-white sari sat on one side of a large set of scales, her face flushed from a mixture of embarrassment and laughter. On the other, the family members and friends waiting by the house placed block after block of golden jaggery, made from sugar cane juice, until the old lady's side of the scales rose up in the air, finally weighing the same as the sweet jaggery bricks on the other side. The old lady smiled a wide, toothless grin as the revelers hooted in celebration.

Ma shook her head. "Can you imagine, making such a spectacle out of an old lady's birthday? And that, too, a widow? Thank God your father isn't here to see this."

I nodded. Babuji was set in his ways and certain he knew what was best for everyone.

Ma headed to the vegetable vendor, and I stuck to her side. He had the day's crop out in wicker baskets all over the side of the path, a tattered canopy of indigo cloth providing a little shade over him and his produce. I was thrilled when Ma started buying okra. She cooked the bhindi with a burst of turmeric, chili powder, and her own blend of spices that she would grind together just before tossing them into the sizzling oil. It was my favorite dish, and no one could make it like Ma. She had tried to teach me several times, but it just didn't taste the same when I made it. It would be yet another item to add to the list of things I would miss about my old life when I moved away from Ma.

Ma put handfuls of okra on the vendor's scale, and the two of them started their usual dance, arguing over the price of the vegetables. Back and forth, bickering, one demanding a lower price, one screaming for a higher price. Ma waved her hand in the man's face, her thin bangles jingling, and turned to pretend she would buy the okra from someone else.

"Was this what it was like?" I asked Ma as the bangles settled on her forearm.

"Shh. He'll lower his price. Just wait."

"Was it?" I asked again as the merchant conceded and gave Ma the price she wanted.

Ma triumphantly poured the okra into her bowl. "What *what* was like, Namak?" she asked, using her strange nickname for me that always embarrassed me in public.

My ears burned out of habit from the nickname that I wished Ma had never come up with, but I remained focused. "When you and Babuji were setting my dowry with Krishna's family," I replied. "Did you argue with them over my worth, like I was nothing but the day's crop?"

Ma stared at me, stunned.

Then behind us, the sound of a man shouting startled us both. We turned.

The screams were coming from a broad-shouldered, fair-skinned British officer ten feet ahead on the path, commanding a marching sepoy unit.

I gasped, dropping the cup, which rolled into the road and right at them. Before I could do anything, Ma pulled me to the side of the cramped path, pressing us up against the baskets of spinach as the sepoys marched toward us.

Sepoys were native Indian soldiers working for the British East India Company. They wore red coats and funny black hats, and their mustaches curled at the ends as they stomped down the narrow market path that wound past my home to Krishna's village and beyond. Their rifles were aimed at the heavens above.

The sepoys and their commander seemed strong and mean. And they were nearing us quickly. I looked down respectfully, holding the part of my sari pallu that went over my head by my cheek. I snuck a few quick glances at the men. I wanted to rush back onto the path and save the cup, the cup that would serve as one of the only reminders of Ma in my new life. But I couldn't get in their way. I could do nothing but watch in horror as the precious cup rolled between the feet of the marching men who were now passing us.

Near the front of the unit, one young sepoy with a long nose stooped out of line, grabbed the cup, and held it out to me. He was tall and clean-shaven, with dimples and gentle eyes like Ma's.

"Charan!" the white man screamed, his face now more pink than white.

The soldier dropped the cup into my hand and stepped back in line. "Sorry, sir!" he replied in Hindi. I began to shake as the British officer puffed his chest out and stormed toward Charan, shouting in English. I couldn't understand a word, yet I knew he wasn't saying nice things.

Ma pulled me back deeper into the market, past the vegetable vendor, whose spinach I almost toppled to the ground. She yanked me to the flour mill behind that stall, away from the sepoys. They continued marching down the path until they were out of sight.

Everyone in the market quickly went back to their business.

"That cup wasn't worth your life, you know," Ma said.

My heart pounded in my chest. "What could I do? The sepoy handed it to me, and I didn't know what to do but take it."

Ma pointed to a sack of wheat flour from the mill. A man in a white kurta and turban working there extended his palm, which was dusted in flour, and Ma paid him.

She lifted the heavy bag of flour and headed back down the same path the sepoys had trod. I followed her. Although the sepoys were long gone, I couldn't stop thinking about the Indian men being ordered around by the British man. I wondered if this was what my life was going to be like in three days—taking orders and having no say.

"You're not Rani Lakshmi Bai," Ma said. Her hold on the basket slipped as she lugged the flour, so she paused to adjust her grip, and then we continued.

Rani Lakshmi Bai was the queen of the faraway kingdom of Jhansi. Although she ruled a couple hundred miles away from us, all of India was talking about her these days, because after her husband died and the British refused to acknowledge her adopted son as the rightful heir to the throne, she took over the throne and started ruling Jhansi herself.

"You're not some strong-willed queen to take on the British. You can't challenge everything, asking questions about your dowry in public," she snapped. "And you can't act like a foolish child anymore, either." She wiped her brow with her forearm. "You're going to have many new responsibilities at your new home."

I took the flour from her, trying to be responsible, although I wasn't sure how to stop acting like a child when I was one. "What if Krishna's mother forces me to work all day? What if she—"

The bag was suddenly smacked out of my hand, sending up a cloud of powdery brown flour as it hit the ground. "Don't eat it! The British have added ground bullock bones to it!" a man shouted. He repeated the message as he ran through the village, spreading the news.

The flour had scattered everywhere, mixing with dry dirt on the ground and leaving just a little in the sack. I lifted what was left of the bag, but Ma put her hand on my wrist. I looked at her, and she shook her head.

"You heard the man," she said. "It has bullock bones in it."

"What a waste," I muttered, patting the flour off my orange blouse.

Ma nodded as we walked up the lane. We were vegetarian. Even though other Hindus did eat some meat, we didn't touch beef. Beef came from cows. Cows plowed the land so we could grow food. They gave us milk so we could make curds and ghee, the purified butter in which we cooked our food and soaked the cotton wicks of our temple lamps. And they gave us fuel when their dung was flattened and dried to later be burned. With all cows did for us, we couldn't eat beef or slaughter them.

"How can it be true, Ma?" I asked, trying to wipe the flour off my hands as we passed the temple and the widows again. "Why would the British do that when it is against our religion?"

"They care about making money off us. They don't care about our religion, Meera. Why do you think those other sepoys mutinied back in the spring?"

"Babuji said the British had given them new rifle cartridges soaked in pig and cow fat, and they had to bite the cartridges to load their weapons," I replied.

"That's right. The British didn't care that if Muslim sepoys bit into pig fat and Hindu sepoys bit into cow fat, they would be going against their religions."

We reached home, where Babuji was still teaching the boys, and headed quietly around my tree to the back of the house, making sure we didn't disturb them.

"These are dangerous times," said Ma as she walked to the lines on which hung our dripping-wet laundry in the humid air. "Be grateful you're married and have someone to take care of you." She placed the okra bowl on the ground, and I followed her lead, putting the cup next to it. She squeezed a few drops of water out of a drying sari over my hands, using it to wipe off the tainted flour.

I watched the beads of water dripping down the edges of the damp clothes, fleeing. "What if . . . what if I don't want to go?" I asked shakily, hoping Ma wouldn't get mad I was questioning things again.

Ma shook the end of the sari to get the new wrinkles out. "What?"

"To Krishna's. What if I'm not grateful that I'm married to him?" I didn't know him. All I knew—from the one word he said in front of me, *namaste*—was that he had winter on his breath, cold and crisp without a hint of warmth, thanks to the little black clove he kept in his mouth all day long to strengthen his teeth.

Ma sighed. "You know, at your wedding—"

"Yes, yes, I know. I had an accident on Babuji's lap."

"No. Not that story, Namak. After that, when the ceremony was over, I started to cry because I couldn't bear the thought of you moving out one day, of losing you too after I lost so many babies. Do you know what your aunt told me?"

I shrugged. "What did Radha Chachi say?"

"Sita Chachi," Ma said, talking about my younger

aunt who had passed away. "Sita told me women were as strong as the sacred fire in the wedding ceremony. That we could grow into a blaze, overcoming any obstacle in our way. But we could also be strong by accepting difficult things. She told me to accept that this was your fate. So now I need you to be strong as fire too and accept that this is happening, because it was decided years ago, and nothing can change that. So accept that it's your duty to go to Krishna's house and be his wife. Can you do that, Meera?"

I didn't answer. I was too busy staring at the water droplets rapidly trickling down the clothes, like they were running for their lives, desperate for a change.

But the same thing happened to each and every one of them when they finally escaped: they plummeted down into the hot, cracked earth and disappeared.

Chapter 2

Later that day, Ma had told me to play outside while she cooked the okra and the rest of dinner. She told me I'd be cooking for the rest of my life, and she wanted me to enjoy my last days at home. So as the sun's beams crept through the window in our tiny earthen home's bedroom, turning the dusty blue paper kite leaning below the window translucent, I left Ma, rushing past the woven cots, turning the corner, and sprinting to the backyard, where I ran my hands along the trunks of the trees I loved to climb. It was strange to think that in a few days, I wouldn't be pulling buckets of water out of the well with Ma. I wouldn't be by her side cooking, singing, hunching over clay vessels as little balls of mustard seed jumped out of the hot oil. And I wouldn't see her smile when she put on her favorite sari, emerald green with paisley embroidery, draping its pallu lovingly over a blouse the color of ripe mangoes.

I raced past our property, following a pair of flying parrots over the hills behind our village, and stopped at the dusty road to Krishna's village, the same road the sepoys marched on when they made their way out of the market. I thought of them getting yelled at by the white officer, the same way Babuji would yell at me if I disturbed his class. I guessed men made the rules in most places, be they Indian or British.

I took a step onto the road at the wide spot where it crossed another winding path. I stared at the cross-roads and couldn't tell from the hundreds of jumbled footprints if the sepoys had gone toward Krishna's village or turned down the other path. I dug my bare foot into the road. Even the sepoys had a choice between several futures. But I had to do what my parents and Krishna's parents had decided for me years ago.

I exhaled as I took in the verdant slopes at the start of Krishna's village. I wanted to see what this future that was chosen for me would be like. So even though I knew Ma would not be happy if she knew what I was doing, I crossed the road and headed up the hill in front of me.

From the hilltop, I could see the rippling river that ran behind both of our villages. I headed down the other side of the hill, toward the dozens of trees at its base right across from Krishna's earthen home, and ducked behind a thick trunk.

A few feet away, Krishna was crouched on the ground outside by his front door, his oily hair parted sharply down the middle. His mother, dressed in a yellow sari, and his older brother, Gopal, in a long mustard kurta and white paijama trousers, were standing over him. I couldn't make out what they were saying. Maybe Krishna wasn't ready for me to move in, either. That could explain his sullen face. Or maybe that was just what he was like all the time. I guessed I would find out soon.

I studied Krishna's mother. I had overheard Ma's friends talking to her at the well when they thought I wasn't listening. Some had married into loving, kind families. But others were miserable, bossed around all day by their mothers-in-law, unable to stand up for themselves because it just wasn't done. I wasn't sure which kind of mother-in-law Krishna's mother would be. But the fact that Babuji was always talking about how their values were so similar to ours made me worry she would be as strict and unwilling to compromise as he was.

A few raindrops fell on my nose, and I watched Krishna's mother dramatically wipe rain off her face like she was swatting mosquitoes away. She patted Krishna and Gopal on the back, and the three of them went inside the house.

I was about to turn back for my village when a flash of blue in the thorny bougainvillea branches caught my eyes. It was a neelkanth, a beautiful jaybird with a bright blue head and wings. Tradition said if you saw one on Dussehra, the holiday celebrating Lord Ram's victory over Ravan, the ten-headed demon king, you would be blessed with a lifetime of good fortune.

I smiled, thinking of my one-year-old little brother's face lighting up when he was the only person in our family who spotted a neelkanth on Dussehra. "Neeka! Neeka!" Ravi had squealed, trying to pronounce the bird's name. Babuji had been so excited Ravi had spotted the bird, he'd had Ma make us sweets to celebrate. Overjoyed that Ravi would be blessed with a lifetime of luck, Ma had happily roasted chickpea flour in ghee, mixing it into round, sugary laddus for us to gobble up.

It was just too bad that Ravi's lifetime of good fortune ended a few weeks after that.

Ravi was everything to us. After I was born, Ma had given birth to three boys in three years—boys who wouldn't cost their family anything like a daughter and her dowry would. But none of them had been born alive.

So when Ravi's screams filled our little house, Babuji had been so surprised he almost spilled his chai all over himself. A boy had finally been born to us, full of life. His hair was thick and dark and as shiny as a crow's wings. His skin was soft, like freshly churned butter. His eyelashes were longer than mine, and with each blink he seemed to be sweeping the past sadness out of my parents' eyes. His birthmark was a blue heart on his shoulder. It was like he was so full of love, one heart wasn't enough.

But early one night in his sixteenth month, he began to throw up and go to the bathroom a lot. Soon his cries became unbearable, but no tears were coming out, and in the lambent light of the lantern, his eyes looked like they were coated in glass. By morning, as the sun warmed our home, Ravi's little body had gone cold. My baby brother was dead from cholera.

Ma cried nonstop the day Ravi died, her nose turning so red and swollen I almost couldn't see the tiny diamond stud she wore in her left nostril. But the next day, she didn't shed a tear. She told me women had to be strong, just like she had this morning. She said they had to be strong enough to handle the discomfort of pregnancy, the pain of childbirth, and the agony of a child's death. Because that was the way things were. She forced me to dry my tears and help her prepare the meals for the day, singing as if nothing had happened. As if the little blue kite lying in the corner of our house, the one Radha Chachi had given us when Ravi was born, wasn't there. As if the little silver rattle, whose handle doubled as a whistle that made Ravi squeal with delight, wasn't lying on its side in silence. As if Ravi had never existed at all.

"Neeka," I whispered to the bird, like my brother.

The neelkanth hopped sweetly from branch to branch, singing its song as a few raindrops sprinkled around it, when suddenly a pebble flew by my ear like a buzzing mosquito, just missing the bird. It shot into the sky, sending magenta blossom petals pouring onto my head like the rains.

"Hey!" I snapped, turning angrily to the perpetrator as the rain started to come down more steadily. "How could you do that—"

I abruptly shut my mouth, trapping the words inside.

It was Shalu, Krishna's sister-in-law . . . my sister-in-law. She was standing at the edge of the yard, where she dropped the handful of pebbles she was clutching. "He was making such a racket," she muttered.

"He was singing," I said softly, hoping no one inside the house could hear me.

Shalu scoffed at me as if I was nothing but a pathetic little girl. I hated feeling that way but knew better than to talk back to my older sister-in-law. Soon I'd be spending every day with Krishna's mother and her.

Maybe it would be like having a sister of my own. Maybe we would have fun. Maybe we would grow close. Maybe I could teach her not to be so mean to birds.

"I'm Meera," I said shakily.

"Krishna's Meera?" Shalu loudly asked, like she was talking about someone's pet dog.

I nodded, hoping she would keep her voice down. Hoping the rest of Krishna's family wouldn't come out of their home next to find me just outside their yard.

Shalu ran her foot through the grass, her silver toe rings, the ones married women wore, glistening. She adjusted the elegant gold-and-black beads of her mangalsutra, the necklace married women wore, and ran her fingers through her hair past the red sindoor in her parting, yet another sign of marriage.

Okay, I thought. *I get it. You're a married woman, and I'm just a little kid.* Even though Shalu was just a year or two older than me, from the looks of it.

"Does Krishna know you're here?" she asked, walking closer.

Rain trickled down my face like tears. I shook my head, not sure what Krishna would say if he caught me trying to spy on his family like this.

Shalu's thick gold bangles, which were carved with elephants, jingled loudly now that she had scared all the birds away. She saw me eyeing them. "Like them? They're one of a kind. From the jeweler in Indranagar, my hometown. What do you think Krishna will change your name to?" she asked, bouncing from one topic to another as flightily as the bird she'd evicted.

I paused. I hadn't thought about it because it wasn't our family's tradition, but some women had to change their names when they got married. Not just their last name—their first name too.

"I'm not Shalu anymore. I'm Sheela. Doesn't it sound so grown up?"

I nodded. When Ma got a new cooking dish every few years, the first thing she would do was have the merchant engrave her name in the metal so everyone would know the dish was hers. This felt like the same thing—only Krishna was the one doing the engraving. My last name would be Krishna's last name. And my first name would be whatever he chose.

Maybe that was why Ma hadn't asked the merchant to engrave the cup she'd given me this morning at the bazaar.

But I liked being Meera. It was *me*.

Shalu's eyes twinkled. "I gave him a suggestion—Shurpanakha."

I frowned. That was the name of Ravan's demoness sister.

Shalu giggled. "I'm just teasing." But there was nothing playful about her laugh. I guessed she wasn't just mean to birds. "He'll name you something nice.

Hopefully." She turned back to the house. "I might still call you 'Shurpanakha,' though," she added, unable to contain her laughter as she ran back to her home that would one day be *our* home.

My cheeks burning, I rushed back over the slick hills for home, wiping the rain from my eyes. Shalu's— Sheela's—voice echoed after me: "Bye, Meera!"

Chapter 3

The next morning, with two days to go until I had to move into Krishna's house, I helped Ma like I always did. While Babuji went for a walk, I gathered flowers for Ma's prayers, collected water with her from the well, helped her stone-grind lentils into flour, cooked breakfast, washed dishes, poured oil into the lamp that rested on an earthen shelf built into our kitchen wall, and finally ate. With everything done, Ma shooed me out the door to join the merriment outside.

And there was a lot of merriment. Because today was a legendary nawab's birthday. Although the ruler had been dead for decades, and his grandson was now a nawab with no power, thanks to the British, the old nawab's birthday was still celebrated here. That was because in the old nawab's time, kites were only for royalty, but he'd allowed villagers to fly them too. And every year on his birthday, he'd fly a kite with gold coins hidden between two layers of paper. It was just a handful of change to him, but it was a fortune for a villager.

So everyone would fly their kites and try to cut others' kites down, hoping to be the lucky soul to cut the nawab's kite. The winner of the kite battle won the loser's kite, and the winner of the nawab's kite would find their destiny changed by the fortune inside it. Though the old nawab was long gone, and there was no treasure to be found in any kite now, we still flew kites and had kite-fighting battles on his birthday. Even Babuji's classes were let off for the festivities.

I headed down the path that swirled through our village and led to the bazaar. Lots of little kids were running toward the stepwell I had gone to earlier with Ma, where people would gather with their kites. Although the only kite we owned was imprisoned in dust and Ma didn't want anyone touching it and possibly damaging one of the few reminders of Ravi we had, it wasn't a problem. Someone or other would always have trouble getting their kite off the ground or get bored. I'd ask to give it a try, and then I'd get a chance to help the shield-shaped kite soar like a bird.

Near the temple, there were now more widows begging outside. I turned to count them and ran smack into Babuji, back from his walk. He was staring at the women.

"Babuji! There are so many widows here today," I sputtered, collecting myself.

"It's the sati ban," Babuji muttered, straightening his white kurta. "I think some are coming here from other villages, like someone else's trash littering our home."

I squeezed my fingers together. I hated how Babuji thought so little of women. "But the ban isn't new," I said. "Sati was outlawed long before Sita Chachi did it."

Babuji nodded, leaning against the ber tree beside him. "I thought the sati abolition movement would never have caught on. But it did. And then the British embraced it too. Forcing their ways on all of us. Giving these foolish women the preposterous idea that they should go on being a burden to their families instead of following their husbands to the afterlife."

It was strange how pink Babuji's ears grew while he complained about how the British thought they were better than us. After all, Babuji thought he was better than girls and women. And Indians had been fighting to stop sati long before the British did. So stopping sati was an Indian belief, not just a British one.

"With Captain Keene enforcing the ban now, more and more people are taking it seriously," he said. "We're lucky you married into one of the few families around that think like we do. The few other chaste families left won't do it. They're too scared of the British." Babuji ran his fingers on the rough bark of the ber tree. "There must be no good women left."

Good women, I thought. *Sati* meant "good woman," someone pure and virtuous. But what was good about having to lose your life on your husband's funeral pyre when you became a widow just so you could join him in the afterlife, like your only purpose was to follow him around? No wonder so few families had practiced sati to begin with, and now, after the ban, even fewer did.

"I get sick to my stomach thinking of the day this tradition ends," Babuji continued.

That's funny, I thought, my eyes turning to stone as I watched my father. *I get sick to my stomach thinking about the day Sita Chachi's life ended.*

It was a couple winters before Ravi was born, when my youngest uncle—Babuji's little brother, Surendra Chacha—passed away in his sleep. Sita Chachi, eight years older than me, who Babuji had treated like a daughter, was already up, heating water in large containers for our showers. When I'd told her the news, she'd broken down. But had she been more upset at Surendra Chacha's passing or at what she was going to have to do in a few hours?

Babuji proudly told anyone who'd listen how little Sita Chachi walked out of our house that evening, head held high, to meet her end on her husband's funeral pyre at the riverbank. But what Babuji didn't mention, what he probably never even noticed, was that Sita Chachi was not happily heading off to fulfill her highest duties as a woman. Sita Chachi was terrified. I was only seven, but even I knew it. The villagers who'd peered into our home to witness the rare spectacle of sati knew it. Ma, who'd held me back, stopping me from grabbing Sita Chachi, knew it. Babuji was oblivious, though. He'd put his hand up to bless my young aunt . . . before leading her to her death.

The last memory I had of my aunt being led away was that her hands were shaking so badly, her bangles clattered. Not melodiously, like the *khun khun* sound poets romanticized. Like teeth rattling in fear. But Babuji just remembered things the way he wanted.

Now Babuji shook his head dismissively at the widows by the temple. "Shameful," he grumbled.

"But what about the rani of Jhansi?" I asked. "Isn't she a good woman? She's a widow ruling a kingdom, and probably making the British really upset."

Babuji's gaze darted around for a split second as he tried to figure out who he thought less of, women or the British colonizers. "There is only one right way, like Sita Chachi, bringing honor to the family." He patted my head. "Now go have fun and fly a kite. Who knows if you'll have time to do it next year, with all the responsibilities you'll have at your new home."

A group of women in brightly colored reds, yellows, and blues ran by us, laughing, as they flew their kites with their kids. Was there a chance I wouldn't be allowed to fly a kite next year because I would be too busy cooking and cleaning for Krishna's family? What other demands would they have? What would they expect me to do later—hopefully *much* later—when Krishna died?

I looked at the widows in white with their hands

out, begging just a few steps from the joyful women and their kites. Nothing seemed fair.

My belly churned at the strange juxtaposition of laughter and sad begging. I had to get away from it. I had to change my path.

I turned abruptly from the road to the well and raced back into our house, plopping onto my woven jute cot. A puff of dust flew into my face, powdering my green sari. The dust particles shimmered in the sunbeam from the window. Ravi's blue kite was just out of reach of the warmth. I turned, trying to ignore it, trying to forget how everything was out of my control, when a breeze from the window tickled the kite, making its paper crinkle.

Scritch, scritch, scritch.

Like it was itching for freedom.

I gently picked up the kite and blew the years of dust off it, sending the particles scattering out the window. The kite fluttered in my fingers, as if unable to resist the call of the wind. It wanted to fly. I wanted to see it fly. And Ravi would have too. So, with the reminder of my brother cradled in my arms, I sprinted outside to the back hills, where the river glistened in the background.

I flicked my wrist and the kite went up, a shield trying to make its way not just to the clouds but *into* them, straight up to the heavens. The sun shone through the kite, giving the blue paper even more brilliance than before.

Blue. The kite in the sky.

Blue. Sweet jaybirds hopping by.

Blue. My brother's second heart.

Blue. Ravi. Now just a tear in my eye.

The kite fluttered, changing directions every now and then when I pulled its string. That poor kite was just like me. Almost free, but not. Happily flying left, then ordered to go right.

In the distance, a red kite was swaying in the wind. I didn't want to lose my brother's kite in a battle. But wasn't flying away better than being trapped inside? I knew the answer, so I jerked the kite forward, my eyes locked on our prey. The red kite flopped closer, unaware, when I suddenly snapped my wrist, twisting my string around its string. I yanked as hard as I could, the tension in my kite string slicing at my fingers until a drop of blood beaded on my palm.

Just like that, the red kite was cut down. I reeled Ravi's kite back in, dragging the tangled kite with it.

"Yes!" I whooped. "I won! I won—"

"Meera!" a voice boomed from behind me. I turned to see Babuji standing there. "Is that . . . is that Ravi's kite?"

Ma rushed to the yard, and I let go of the kite string, but there was no hiding what I had done. The reel was by my feet, and the kites were falling down right above me. Before Babuji could yell at me, another scream erupted.

I looked up. A small figure was running over the hill toward us, shouting and sobbing, his teary face glistening as much as his oily hair. It was Krishna.

"Why did you do that?" he shouted, his face glistening with sweat. Well, this was certainly more than "namaste." I glanced at Babuji as Krishna shouted.

"You can't cut down my kite, Meera! Who do you think you are? That was *my* kite! My best kite! And now look at it! It's torn! It's bent! It's—"

"You can have this one," Babuji said, catching the blue kite and handing it to Krishna.

"That's Ravi's kite!" I said, as if my father needed the reminder.

Babuji gave me a sharp look, the vein in the center of his forehead sticking out like an earthworm on dry land, and Ma, now by my side, shook her head, begging me to be quiet.

Krishna took the blue kite and snapped it in half.

"No!" I wailed at the mangled kite, which he threw to the ground.

"I don't need your cheap kite. I'm going to Delhi today to pick up my cousins. I'll get something much better than this." Krishna stormed down the hill, the angry shouts of his tantrum still audible. I stared in shock at the weeping, snotty mess disappearing behind the slopes.

The red kite didn't bring with it riches for my future. It brought Krishna, my actual future.

And my future was full of tears.

Chapter 4

A green flower filled my palm as the afternoon sun filtered in through our sitting room windows. But this time it wasn't a flower I picked from a garden for Ma's puja. With just a day to go before my thirteenth birthday, Ma was drawing a flower design on my palm from a paste of henna leaves.

Despite its strong, earthy odor, mehendi was always refreshing, especially in the summer months leading up to the monsoon when the heat was almost intolerable. The henna had a cooling effect, so as soon as it was applied, my palms started to feel like I was on a frosty mountain in Kashmir with a handful of snow.

"Look at you! My little baby, all grown up!" sniffled a voice in the doorway. It was Radha Chachi, my aunt. My overly emotional aunt. She and my uncle had just arrived from their home in Delhi to see me off.

"You made it!" Ma exclaimed. "We were so worried." She gave my aunt a warm hug.

I started to get up, to bow at Chacha's and Chachi's feet for blessings, but there was no way I could put my hands together in a namaste without ruining the mehendi, which had several hours to go before it was dry.

"Let it be, beta," said Hari Chacha, setting down his cotton sack full of clothes.

"If you let one thing slide, then another tradition will go, and pretty soon the next generation will start thinking they're British," Babuji muttered.

Ma shook her head at Babuji's words as Radha Chachi rushed to my side to get a better look at my hands. She pinched my cheeks and hugged my head. "I can remember the day you were born." Big tears began to spill down her high cheekbones, briefly pooling in her dimples before they spilled over onto her neck. "I helped deliver you, you know."

I nodded, forcing a smile. Radha Chachi and Hari Chacha used to live with us. But after my other uncle's death and Sita Chachi's sati, they had moved to the big city of Delhi. They were like second parents to me, and were not at all as strict as Babuji was. But the journey from Delhi to our village was so difficult, the roads patrolled by dacoits and thugs, thieves and bandits who were looking for any chance to rob you, that we only saw each other once a year now at Diwali.

Radha Chachi wailed dramatically. I hated the sound of her cries, like a donkey in agony. The last time I'd heard them was when Ravi passed away. She had cried so much that Babuji had insisted she and Chacha head back to Delhi early. I wasn't sure if it was because she was making us so much sadder than we already were or if it was because she was hurting Babuji's ears.

"She's just emotional today," my uncle explained as Babuji raised an eyebrow at the sound. "The East India Company is taking back Delhi. There are riots everywhere."

"We heard," Ma said. "I can't believe the rebels could even hold the city for so long."

Delhi was one of the biggest cities under the British East India Company's control. Rebels had taken it back from the British in May, and we were lucky to not have had any violence spillover here, but who knew if we'd be that lucky again. The riots we'd been hearing news of could easily spread to the neighboring villages. To our village.

"So many screams," Radha Chachi continued. "The night was even darker with the smoke from all the fires."

Hari Chacha shuddered. "At least there wasn't an explosion this time, like when the rebels blew up the magazine in May."

"What's a magazine?" I asked.

"The building near the sepoy barracks," my aunt replied, "where the British keep all their canons and cartridges—"

Babuji cleared his throat loudly.

I frowned. If I wasn't old enough to hear about riots and magazines exploding, maybe Babuji should have realized I wasn't old enough to move out. Or to be married.

"Anyway, forget all that." Radha Chachi quickly changed the subject. "Soon our little Meerabai will be united with her Krishna!"

I tried to smile. The real Meerabai had passed away hundreds of years ago. She'd married a prince, but he'd died on the battlefield. Meerabai had refused to commit sati. She'd refused to listen to what her dead husband's family wanted her to do. Instead, she'd made her own destiny and became a traveling poet, singing about her devotion to God, to Lord Krishna.

I stared at my hands as Radha Chachi squeezed my shoulders. Soon the green paste would harden and fall off, leaving behind an orange design on my skin.

The stain would fade away in a few days. But reality wouldn't. Krishna, the crying poor sport without a hint of warmth would be a permanent part of my life—unless I did something about it.

Chapter 5

The riots didn't spread to our village. But by that evening, as the sun started to go down, the village dogs
were restless, and their haunting howls made the
already humid monsoon air feel even heavier. From
where they stood by the windowsill in our bedroom,
Radha Chachi and Ma seemed unaffected. They
had already scrubbed the hardened remains of the
mehendi off their own hands that they had put on
each other after mine was done. Now, holding my
wrists out the window, they poured a little well water
left from the morning over my hands to remove the
dried paste. They began making all sorts of cooing
noises, admiring the rich orange color of the mehendi
design.

For Ravi's first Diwali, Radha Chachi brought us two tiny wooden dolls from Delhi. I remembered how much fun I'd had putting my doll in the fancy red-and-gold sari Chachi had sewn for it. That must have been what Ma and Chachi were feeling now as they practiced putting my hair up, made me change into my own red-and-gold sari, and made last-minute adjustments on the blouse, tucking and sewing and giggling like a major city wasn't burning.

I stood before our wooden armoire and tugged at the bun Ma had tied too tightly. A set of red glass bangles clinked noisily against one another on my wrists.

Ma had taken out one of my grandmother's old cotton saris and wrapped all my clothes inside it before tying it into a sack for me to take to Krishna's house the next day. The indigo pouch filled with my dowry sat next to the sack on my cot, along with some wedding jewelry for me to wear tomorrow, safe until my parents needed to deliver everything, along with me, in the morning. Ma slid two silver toe rings onto my feet. My aunt reached for the tiny jewelry pile and pulled out the mangalsutra, the necklace I'd be wearing every day after tomorrow to show I was a married woman. She clasped a little gold hook onto an even tinier gold hoop, latching the mangalsutra around my neck like she was finalizing my destiny.

I looked in the mirror, wondering what Shalu—no, Sheela—would think of my simple mangalsutra with much smaller gold beads than hers. I hoped that by tomorrow she would have forgotten to call me Shurpanakha and prayed the name Krishna picked for me was nothing like that.

Maybe he'll be too busy crying about his kite still to change my name, I thought, irritated.

In that moment, a loud shout came from outside. It sounded like it was coming from the back hill. The village dogs started barking aggressively. Then a woman's sob wailed across the hill. Ma and Radha Chachi exchanged worried glances.

"Is it the riots?" I asked. Maybe they had finally spread to our village. Maybe tomorrow's events would be postponed. Or better yet, canceled altogether. Not that I *wanted* a riot to come to our village. I didn't know what a riot even consisted of. Fire and smoke and screaming, from what Chachi had mentioned. I guessed it wasn't something to really wish for.

Ma headed out our room's narrow double doors to the tiny hall, where Babuji and Chacha had been sitting on cots, drinking their evening chai. No one was there now.

Radha Chachi smiled at me as the doors swung back and forth, squeaking on their hinges. "It will be okay."

I ran to the window behind me and peeked out, craning my neck. There was a crowd of people at the side of our house, including Krishna's parents, Babuji, and Chacha. I saw Ma rush over to them. Everyone was talking at once, and I couldn't tell what was going on, but I wondered if Krishna had told them about his kite. Were they demanding we pay for a new one?

The crowd dispersed, and Ma burst back into our room, her eyes wide. "What is it?" I asked as a flash of lightning lit up the little patch of sky in the window.

"Krishna went to the city yesterday with his father," replied Ma, gripping the doorframe for support.

"I know that. Is this about the kite? Do they want us to pay for whatever he bought in the city?" I couldn't believe it. Krishna really *was* still crying about it. And now I was going to have to live with him and hear him go on and on about how I cut his kite and how he bought a new one when I probably wouldn't even be allowed to fly a kite with all the work his grumpy mother was going to make me do?

But Ma just shook her head, taking a few steps toward me and Radha Chachi. "It's not that," she said, reaching for my hand. "On his way there, he got caught in the riots, Namak. Krishna is dead."

Krishna was dead.

I wasn't going to have to wear this mangalsutra anymore. I wasn't going to have to watch Sheela throw stones at helpless little birds. I wasn't going to have to take orders from Krishna's mother tomorrow. And best of all, I wouldn't have to leave Ma.

But Ma didn't seem as happy as I was. Her hand trembled in mine. I frowned, feeling sick. I didn't like Krishna, and I had been desperate for a way out of having to live with him tomorrow, but I'd never wanted him to pass away.

All I could think of was that soggy little clove he kept in his mouth all day. It must have been under his tongue when he died. And I wondered, with his last wintry breath, if the rest of his body also turned to ice. Cold and quiet like a December night.

I knew what it was like to lose someone. I didn't want Krishna's mother to feel what Ma and I had felt when Ravi died.

Ma's whole body started to shake as she began

to cry so intensely there wasn't even a sound, except when she gasped painfully for air. Was she thinking about Ravi too?

"It's okay, Ma," I said, hugging her. I knew it was wrong to feel so relieved when she must be grieving anew for my little brother, but as awful as this was for Krishna and his family, a weight left me I hadn't realized I'd been carrying.

Ma clenched me tightly as if she would never let me go.

"I know it's sad, Ma. I feel bad for Krishna's mother too. But why are you getting this upset? I don't have to leave tomorrow anymore. We can be together. We can cook together. We can go to the market together. We can—"

"Don't you see, Meera? Krishna is *dead*." The words shivered out of Ma.

I looked at her eyes glistening with sorrow and panic.

"*Your husband* is dead. That makes you a widow." Ma took a deep breath before dissolving into tears again. "His family just came here to tell us the news. I begged them to reconsider. To let you live out the rest of your life as a widow in white at their home. But they refused. I told your father to do something. But he wouldn't. He said this is the way things are, and he couldn't stop this even if he wanted to, which he didn't. You're their daughter-in-law. They make the decisions, and he fully agrees with what they have decided."

My insides felt like they were folding over.

Radha Chachi sank to the cot. "This can't be happening again," she cried.

I looked at her, my legs wobbly, as Ma continued.

"Krishna's family doesn't want to dishonor Krishna, Meera. They don't want people thinking his wife isn't good, dutiful, and devoted. They don't want Krishna to be alone."

No. This wasn't happening. It couldn't be happening. "You're scaring me, Ma," I whispered.

"I'm scared too, but we have no choice. You have to follow Krishna." Ma sobbed, biting her lip. "You have to commit sati, Meera."

Chapter 6

*W*ith the last dying rays of sunlight barely visible on the horizon, Krishna's funeral procession had already begun. Dozens of mourners from his village would have been carrying a cot bearing his body, covered in a white cotton cloth with just the face visible, heading right for the riverbank bordered by our villages for his final rites. I was running out of time to ensure they weren't my final rites too.

As the rest of my family watched, I fell at Babuji's feet in the hall, trying not to vomit. "You said it yourself, Babuji. So many Indians are against sati, and Captain Keene is enforcing the ban. Why risk getting in trouble?"

"I'll risk getting into trouble with the law any day if it means defending my beliefs and our honor."

Babuji was unwavering, his eyes narrowing into dark little tamarind seeds.

Hari Chacha put his hand on Babuji's shoulder and opened his mouth like he was trying to figure out what he could respectfully say to his older brother to stop this. But before he could say a word, Babuji shook Chacha's hand off. His voice rose.

"This is what my father taught me. And this is what you have been taught, Meera. You are a wife. A virtuous wife must go with her husband when he passes and join him in the afterlife. What else would you do? Beg outside a temple and bring disgrace to the family? What kind of a life is that?"

The faint smell of burning sandalwood wafted through the window. Was it Krishna's pyre, made of wood and a tiny bit of camphor and sandalwood, burning on the distant shore? Was it starting before I even got there? I wasn't sure, but never had the calming, perfumed scent of sandalwood felt so sickening.

My words quivered as I joined my palms in a namaste and looked up at my father, searching for a way to convince him he was wrong. "But . . . Rani Lakshmibai is a widow, and she is a queen ruling a kingdom. Meerabai was a widow, and she became a singing poet whose words are so beautiful we still sing her songs today. Think of what we would have lost if they'd just given up their lives because their husbands died."

"You're not a queen. And you're not a poet. You're just a girl. An ordinary girl. Do you think Krishna's family will happily care for you for decades, knowing you didn't commit sati and brought shame to their family name?" Babuji retorted.

"Babuji, please." My throat tightened. It wasn't fair. So what if I wasn't a poet or a queen? Didn't I deserve to live too? Why should my life be taken away from me because someone else died? Why was my worth attached to Krishna? Why was I nothing without him? "We don't know anyone other than Sita Chachi who had to do this. No one in our village does it. So few families even believe in sati to begin with—"

"Just because everyone is doing something wrong doesn't make it right. And this is what Krishna's family wants. It's what your husband's family wants, so you must listen."

"But if I had been married into another family, this wouldn't even be happening. Please!"

"I know it is scary," Babuji said, patting my head. "But this is what is right, Meera. Now be brave and go wait in the bedroom until someone from Krishna's family comes to get you. No more crying. I will *not* have this become a village spectacle again."

"No . . ." I whimpered. This was not happening. I was not going to lose my life because of Krishna. That wasn't fair.

My legs felt as stable as mud as Radha Chachi and Ma helped me to my weak feet. I walked the few steps to the bedroom with their help. I glanced at my cold and clammy hands, still smaller than Ma's, remembering hearing about a palace in Rajasthan that had dozens of small handprints in clay on their walls. They were the handprints of all the child brides who'd had to commit sati when the old king died. I wasn't even important enough to have my handprint memorialized for people to remember me by.

As I stepped into the room, I glanced back at Babuji in the sitting room, who stood tall, fists clenched. It was the same unwavering pose he had taken when he led Sita Chachi to the funeral pyre. I wiped my hands on my sari. I was *not* going to disappear like one of those drops of water from the clothesline.

I turned to Ma as she locked the doors behind us. "Why won't you do something?"

"These are our beliefs, Meera," she said shakily, sounding like Babuji's trained parrot. "These are your husband's family's beliefs."

"These beliefs are wrong!" I sobbed.

Radha Chachi began her donkey cries in the corner by the armoire. I didn't feel happy to have someone crying over my death before I was even gone. It made me even angrier at Ma.

"All you did was beg Krishna's mother to save me? What happened to being as strong as fire?" I shouted. "You shouldn't be begging. You should be fighting for me, fierce as flame, blazing, raging, putting a stop to this."

"I am strong," Ma replied, her eyes lifeless. "That's how I will be able to bear the loss of you, my dearest child."

"Your *only* child," I snapped between tears. "You will have no one when I'm gone."

Ma bit her lip as she quickly turned and left the room.

Radha Chachi locked the door again behind Ma and put her arm around me, patting my shoulder and squeezing it as she dabbed my face with her sari pallu. "She doesn't want you to see her cry."

Ma had no problem crying in front of me just a few minutes ago, I thought, ignoring Radha Chachi's attempt to console me. Faint wafts of smoke drifted through the open window. It was almost time for someone to come take me to my fate. For my mother and father to let them lead me to my end.

The thought of flaming logs on my skin made my whole body feel sweaty. I suddenly heard the haunting clinking of Sita Chachi's bangles.

I looked down at my hands. It was the sound of *my* bangles. My hands shook as I looked at my aunt. "I'm scared."

There was a knock at the door. I knew that knock. Harsh and piercing. It was Babuji.

"Just a minute," Radha Chachi called out, dragging the cot holding my dowry over to the window. She climbed on the bed and peeked outside.

Babuji knocked louder. "It's time."

"We're coming!" Radha Chachi jumped down, grabbed my hand, and led me to the cot instead of the door. "Go," she whispered, motioning to the window.

"What?"

"Go!" she hissed, grabbing the indigo pouch with my dowry and the cotton sari sack with my clothes and shoving them in my hands. "Like the real Meerabai. Quickly."

Somehow, the possibility of living scared me even more. "He'll never forgive you."

Radha Chachi smiled through her tears. "I helped you come into this world. I'm not going to help you leave it. You won't end up like your Sita Chachi. Go. Now!"

I squeezed my aunt's hand, regretting ever comparing her to a donkey. I pulled the skirt of my wedding sari up high enough to hop onto the cot and climb out the window.

As my bare feet hit the dirt, I heard the bedroom door open and Babuji shout upon discovering I wasn't inside. It was now or never. I had to run like my life depended on it.

Because it did.

Chapter 7

The chirps of the crickets, the croaks of the frogs, the hoots of the owls, all the sounds that I'd once loved to fall asleep to—they all sounded terrifying under the moonless night. I clumsily sprinted through the village, my anklets jingling as I ducked behind bullock carts, sleeping donkeys, crumbling gray walls, and little homes whenever I spotted a person.

I unhooked my anklets and clenched them in my fist to silence them against the bundle I carried. I needed to get out of the village, but which way was I supposed to go? Which way would be safe?

If I went west, I would hit Krishna's village. That was definitely off-limits, unless I wanted to be forced onto his pyre by his female relatives, angry I had shamed their family name by trying to run from my sacred duty. If I went north, I'd end up on the riverbank where the pyre was, lying in wait for me with his male family members. If I went east, I'd have to run through our entire village. It was too risky.

So I went south, down the winding path along the edge of the village, not even caring that I might run right into a marching column of sepoys. I just kept running, my feet hitting the hard ground until I was past the outer limits of our village.

The smells of the pyre were no longer noticeable here. I was far from the funeral. But not far enough. As buzzing mosquitoes circled me, I searched the darkness for where to go next, feeling around me until I ran into the tall grass and cluster of trees that grew alongside the river where it bent south. If I could get through the patch of trees, I could reach the river and follow it farther southeast. Farther from the pyre. Farther from my death.

A voice bounced through the wooded field. "Meera!"

I froze. It was Babuji's voice. I crouched behind a tree trunk, picturing his vein pulsating angrily on his forehead. I had to get the rest of my noisy jewelry off, or I'd be found in no time. And without any visible jewelry, hopefully I would be of no use to any dacoits or thugs that found me, either.

So I quickly unhooked my mangalsutra, clenching the jewelry tightly, and removed the toe rings, so their ends wouldn't poke me as I ran.

"Meera!" Babuji screamed. "There's still time. Don't do this!"

My hands were sweaty from nerves, and I fumbled with the knot of the indigo pouch, but it finally opened. I put the jewelry in it, then shoved the pouch deep into the cotton sari sack holding my clothes to totally muffle the sound. As I did all this, I crouched in the plants and slunk away from the direction of his voice.

But my glass bangles started clinking together loudly.

I pulled at them as I kept moving forward, trying to tug them over my wrists. My hands were swollen from all the running, though, and the tight bangles were stuck.

There was just one thing I could do. I reached around in the dark, flicking a crawling centipede off my hand. I sorted through the damp dirt until I found a large enough rock and pressed the rock hard against the glass bangles, splitting them silently. With the bangles cracked, I was able to break them off my arm. I cut myself here and there but ignored the pain. Because at least now, I'd no longer sound like someone's lost cow with a bell on its neck when I ran.

As a flash of lightning split the sky, illuminating me for a brief second, I quickly tied the cotton sari sack to my left shoulder and stood tall. Then I pushed forcefully through the grass and trees, my feet getting jabbed by sticks and rocks, my arms and hands and cheeks getting scratched by the bark. I squeezed my eyes shut so they wouldn't get poked by any branches and continued forward.

"Meera!" Babuji's screams drifted toward me with the breeze as rain started to fall down. "Meera, what kind of life will you lead as a widow? Come back!"

Come back so I could die? My eyes snapped open. I didn't know what kind of life I'd be leading as a widow, but at least I would be alive. Ignoring all the jabs and pokes, I started to run even faster through the downpour, gasping for air, racing from that future I had no say in, the future that Babuji was so eager to have come to pass.

Rain soaked my sari, making it harder to run, and the steady downpour kept me from seeing more than a few inches ahead, but I kept going. I found my way out of the shadowy cluster of trees, crossed a road, and raced through another grassy field, and another and another—huffing, running, fleeing, until Babuji's screams were just a memory in the wind.

Exhausted, I paused, my toes gripping at the loose, soaked soil around me. Over the sound of the rain shower, I could hear the river somewhere ahead in the darkness. Raindrops pattered my face as I tilted my face to the sky and caught my breath.

I had escaped. I had actually escaped. I was going to get to see my thirteenth birthday tomorrow. Whatever life had in store for me, I was going to live—

Then a hand covered my mouth, and an arm wrapped around my shoulders. "Don't move," a voice hissed in my ear.

This wasn't happening. I hadn't gotten this far from the pyre to lose my life at the hands of a dacoit. I struggled, trying to pull the hand off me, when the robber raised a lantern to my face.

"Don't I know you?" he whispered, releasing me.

I gasped. It was no dacoit. It was Sepoy Charan,

dressed in the red coat of his sepoy uniform, just like when he'd handed me back my cup in the market.

If one sepoy was here, the rest of them were sure to be nearby. I had to get away. I tried to move, trapped by his hand and my sari pouch, which seemed to be stuck under his arm while still tied to me.

I pushed him hard and turned to run, but my foot slipped in a gush of wet mud, and I skidded down an incline. But I didn't land on the ground—I fell into the muddy river and was being swept downstream, thanks to the rain.

I started to swim, hoping I could get back to shore and not lose my belongings. But my sari sack with my jewelry and the two saris I owned slipped off and started to float away from me. Then my wedding sari started weighing me down. My legs got twisted in the fabric, and I started to sink.

Sepoy Charan dove in after me. In the dying light of his lantern floating nearby, I could see flashes of his red uniform through the rain.

I tried to keep my head above water, but I was bobbing over and over and over, wheezing, choking, panicking . . . and then everything went dark.

Chapter 8

I coughed hard, and river water spilled down my neck.

"See? I told you she'd be okay," said a girl's voice.

Lying on my back on rocking wood, I squinted in the darkness and let out a few more coughs. The oarsman picked up a lantern, and as its light shone brighter and wider, I could see a girl leaning in toward me, about my age with a face as round as the moon and hair plaited into two long braids. Behind her was Sepoy Charan and an older man and woman seated with shawls around their heads and torsos, resting against each other as they slept.

I was on a boat about seven feet long, from what little I could see. The rain had let up, but everything was still slick, including my hair and clothes. Luckily it was still warm enough that I wasn't shivering, although I did feel a little chilly. I winced and sat up slowly, my hands slipping on the wet planks of wood as I almost bumped into the oarsman standing behind me, rowing the boat through the shadowy river.

"You saved me," I sputtered, trying to breathe without choking.

"We all did," the girl replied, motioning to the oarsman and Charan, who was lighting his lantern again with the wick from the oarsman's lamp. "We can do a lot when we work together." She frowned at Sepoy Charan as his revived flame swayed on the wick. "And you could do a lot more if you didn't take orders from the British."

Charan seemed startled by her blunt words. He frowned but then let out a small laugh. "Some people have no choice but to work for them, Bhavani," he said to her. "They need money to survive, and the East India Company controls the money in this area."

"Because they're thieves, looting us and our land just to benefit themselves." Bhavani cleared her throat as a larger boat approached, filled with sacks and sacks of grain illuminated by lantern light.

"See?" She gestured to the boat as it went past us.

"Stealing our food supply. Forcing farmers to only sell their grain to them. You know, they tax weavers in my village for producing their beautiful fabrics, and then use the weavers' own money from those taxes to buy their work for free? The poor weavers cut off their own thumbs so they wouldn't have to work for nothing for the British anymore."

Charan didn't reply, and the air was filled with the sound of frogs croaking around us.

"Anyway," Bhavani continued, "when we found you, you said you were ambushed by rebels and got lost when you found her." She pointed to me. "But I don't see your East India Company out searching for you. Where are your other sepoys? You'd be stuck on the other side of the river in the storm, nowhere near your barracks, if it weren't for us."

Charan lowered his voice. "It's good to have a fire inside you. Don't ever let anyone douse it. But these are dangerous times. You don't need to be so open about your feelings for the British. You don't know who you can trust around these parts."

A shiver ran down my back as he crouched beside me, causing the boat to wobble even more than it already was. "This boat is going the opposite direction of your village, to Indranagar," he said.

"Where he will sleep nicely in his barracks, thanks to us," Bhavani added.

My belly gurgled nervously. Indranagar was a tiny city controlled by the East India Company, where the British officials lived in bungalows run by dozens of Indian servants.

"We're not making any detours," Bhavani replied, her voice unwavering as she handed me my soaked sari sack. Someone had saved it!

I clenched it, squeezing out water and feeling for the indigo pouch inside. I breathed a sigh of relief when my fingers grazed the hard ridges of the jewelry still safe inside. Now I had to make sure I was safe too. "I left for a reason. I don't want to go back there," I said softly.

"Good," Bhavani said. "I've been traveling for months and worked hard to earn enough money to get here. Nothing's going to get in my way. Not a runaway girl, and certainly not the East India Company." Her expression hardened as she eyed Charan's uniform.

"My name's Meera," I said, hugging the sari sack. "Are those your parents?"

"Shh!" the woman hissed from the far end of the little boat.

"We're trying to sleep," grumbled the man, pulling the shawl farther over his face to avoid seeing or hearing us.

"I'm alone," Bhavani whispered to me. "They're just passengers on the boat like all of us. My mother passed away long ago, and my father just died, so I'm here to find my older sister, Chhaya didi."

"I'm sorry," I said, thinking how sad I would feel if my parents passed away, before suddenly remembering how my parents had acted when I was going to pass away. I cleared my throat. "Does your sister live there with her husband?" I asked softly, afraid the sleepy couple would snap at me again.

Bhavani shook her head. "She's not married. She's an ayah for someone in the town, taking care of some British family's little girl. I need to find her and tell her what happened to our father."

I nodded as Bhavani scooched closer to me and rested her head on my drenched shoulder like we were old friends. She handed me a folded-up leaf before closing her eyes to sleep.

As the boat continued rocking down the river, I opened the rubbery leaf and found a tiny handful of rice with cooked lentils on top. I scooped it up with my fingers and bit in. It was cold and tasteless and nothing like Ma's cooking. But it had been so many hours since my last meal, and all that running had made me hungry, so I savored the food all the same, even if it had no salt.

I blinked hard at the thought of salt—namak. Ma used to tell me I was the salt in her life. It was our inside joke and one of Ma's favorite stories to tell. Lord Krishna had two wives. He told one of them she was like sugar. But when the other wife asked, "If she is sugar, what am I?" Krishna replied, "Salt." The wife was hurt by his answer. That night, Lord Krishna hosted a feast at his palace for hundreds of guests. They began to gobble up their food but suddenly started gagging. The food was awful. Krishna had told the cooks to make it without any salt, to show his second wife just how important she was to him.

Ma used to always threaten to make food without salt when I would pretend to be hurt by her calling me the salt of her life. If only Ma had actually tasted how bad this unsalted food was, she would never make that joking threat again.

Shivering in my wet clothes, I fought back tears, thinking of how Ma would never call me Namak again. I didn't care how silly the nickname was. I didn't care that nobody else would ever call someone salt as a nickname. I would have given anything to hear her call me that again. But that was impossible. I'd never see her again. I hugged the sari we had practiced our embroidery on tight, running my fingers over the bumpy stitches in the flowers and paisley designs we had created.

Feeling as rocky and unsure of my future as the unsteady boat we were on, I closed my eyes and went to sleep, ready for this nightmare to end.

Chapter 9

"*We're here,*" *Bhavani said,* shaking me awake on the morning of my thirteenth birthday.

Everything was still dark, but a few birds were already chirping. I yawned, remembering how Ma had woken me on my last birthday. There had been a strange chirping outside, and she hadn't wanted me to miss out on seeing a rare bird. We had rushed out the door, but it wasn't some undiscovered species. It was a sparrow. And the only reason we hadn't recognized its calls was because they were cries of distress. A cat had taken the sparrow's chick out of her nest and was playing with the injured baby. The poor sparrow was so distraught she'd dived at the cat, squawking at it to leave her baby alone.

Later, after I had eaten my special birthday lunch of bhindi with steaming rounds of whole wheat roti, the sparrow was still crying behind the cat, determined to make its life miserable for killing her chick.

A little bird was able to fight that hard for her child, risking her own life in the process. Yet my own mother had not spoken up when I was in danger.

A small wave splashed the side of the boat, snapping me back to the present. The strong scent of fish lingered around us as the boat docked, and the grouchy couple got off. There were a couple of small homes with wooden boats resting against them that I could just barely make out on the shore of Indranagar. In the distance, I could see dozens and dozens of taller buildings and canopies, some illuminated by tiny flickering lanterns that were twinkling like the stars peeking through the clouds above us.

I was so far from my village, no one would ever think to find me here. I stood up, my clothes still slightly wet, and turned to thank the oarsman for saving me and letting me cross the river. Bhavani hopped off onto shore. Charan held the lantern up so I could see and waited patiently while I took a shaky, unsure step forward, getting to land.

Then Charan got off the boat, handing over some wet coins from his pocket to the oarsman. "For the girl too." The oarsman gave him a namaste. "Remember," Charan said to us, "be strong. But be safe. Not everyone takes kindly to words of rebellion."

I nodded, and Charan walked past us to leave. But then he paused, briefly illuminating the handful of tiny homes where the fishermen and fisherwomen slept, and turned back to hand me the lantern. "I know how to get where I'm going. Looks like you're still finding your way," he said, the corner of his mouth curling up into a smile.

I took the lantern, and he ran off into the darkness. "I don't know what to do," I said to Bhavani, hating that I sounded so unconfident and uncertain all the time.

"Sleep," Bhavani said, walking up to a lone tree next to the homes. She lay down to sleep on the wet ground. "You can figure it out in a bit when the sun comes up."

I walked toward Bhavani and glanced around at the homes. Would the people who lived there be upset when the sun came up and they saw us here? I was unsure if this was a good idea, but Bhavani seemed to know what she was doing, so I put the lantern down and rested my head on the wet sari pouch stuffed with reminders of my old life. I closed my eyes. But my heart and my mind were still racing from what had happened hours earlier. I didn't know that I could figure out how to survive without Ma or even Babuji telling me what to do. I didn't know if I had enough money. I had my dowry, but that wouldn't be enough to purchase land for a home, would it?

Too bad I hadn't gone to school or been taught any of these things. My parents had assumed I would just go live at Krishna's. I didn't even know if the money I had would last me long enough to go farther south to find land to buy. We were far from Babuji and Krishna's family, but who knew what kind of people lived in this town? Who lived in the tall buildings just beyond the little homes here? And who was roaming around the paths and alleys up ahead? Were there dacoits and thugs in Indranagar? Were we safe sleeping out in the open here?

I shivered at a slight breeze on the backs of my arms and opened my eyes. Everything was dark. The lantern was gone. What if it really was a thug or a dacoit? I sat up suddenly, turning to wake Bhavani.

But I couldn't feel anyone lying next to me anymore.

I saw the faint glow of the lantern up ahead. I stood up quickly with my belongings, hoping I wasn't following her as she was going to the bathroom. That would have been embarrassing for both of us.

But Bhavani wasn't crouching down somewhere to relieve herself. She was walking past the handful of small homes with boats and fishing nets draped outside them, down the dirt road that Charan had run off on. Crickets were chirping all around us. Some insect or snake was hissing. The tall buildings up ahead seemed to loom over us, and I walked a little faster, trying to catch up, my feet now stinging with each step on the rain-dampened ground. Then I stepped on a broken reed.

"Ouch!" I muttered, unable to stop myself.

Bhavani stopped by some jasmine bushes in front of a crumbling building with arched windows and looked back. "Why are you following me?" she asked softly. "I'm trying to find my sister."

"In the dark? With my lantern?"

Bhavani turned down a wider dirt road and passed a bunch of sleeping goats tied to a tree. "She's working for someone in the East India Company. Maybe it's an official. Maybe it's a collector. I don't know. She left us long ago to find a job here. She would send word to us through people traveling that she was fine and working as an ayah, taking care of a little girl. That's all I know, and this is a big town. So I need to start searching."

"You're just a girl, alone in this big place," I said, wincing at my sore feet as I limped behind Bhavani. The lantern lit up the steely gaze in her eyes.

"Just a girl?" Bhavani said a little harshly, turning to face me. "There are places in this land where women are in charge of the family, where husbands leave their childhood homes to move into their wives' homes, where people *celebrate* when a girl is born. There are schools for girls. There's a queen defending her kingdom. You have no idea what a girl is capable of."

I crossed my arms. I wasn't so sheltered that I didn't know who the rani of Jhansi was. "So why not wait until the sun rises?" I huffed, taking in bits and pieces of dozens and dozens of homes and buildings off in the distance with flickering lanterns, just barely visible in the dark. The tall buildings blocked much of my view. "Like you told me to do?" I twisted my lips. Instead of taking her own advice, here she was taking my lantern and abandoning me. But I had to tread carefully. I didn't want to risk making Bhavani angry enough to actually leave me here by myself.

Bhavani groaned. "Look, don't take this the wrong way, but I didn't want to have you tagging along. That's why I thought I'd get a head start now. I have enough to worry about and don't need to stress about having to take care of you too."

I bit the insides of my cheeks, offended. "I don't need anyone to take care of me," I muttered, not sure I believed what I was saying.

"Right. Because you were doing such a great job of it yourself, almost drowning in a river and making friends with a sepoy."

My aching toes clenched the dirt below. I was tired of people thinking I was weak and needed to be cared for. I was tired of people thinking I wasn't important enough or intelligent enough or strong enough to survive with Krishna gone. I was tired of thinking it myself.

In reality, though, I was a little scared to be sleeping out in this new town by myself in the dark. I was nervous at the thought of having to find a way to survive alone. I didn't know Bhavani well, but at least I knew her. I'd be safer with her until I could earn enough money to buy some land somewhere and start my life.

"I'm not as weak as you think. My in-laws wanted me to commit sati. I wanted to live. So I ran," I said, gritting my teeth as my feet began to burn with pain, almost like I was on a hot funeral pyre.

"Sati?" Bhavani asked, the disgust showing in her crumpled mouth. "I didn't think anyone actually did that."

I seethed all over as I thought about Krishna's family trying to lead me to my own end, about my parents letting it happen. My life being deemed unlivable and unworthy just because Krishna had died. "I don't need anyone to take care of me," I said again over the noise of the crickets, trying to force myself to believe it too. "But I can help you find your sister."

"How? You don't even know what she looks like."

"I know what a little girl looks like. I can help you ask around. It will be faster that way, won't it? Didn't you say something about accomplishing a lot when you work together?"

Bhavani twisted her lips and threw her head up toward the starlit sky, sighing. Then she handed me the well-worn sandals off her feet.

I took them hesitantly. "What are these for?"

"Your feet must hurt from all that running." Bhavani paused. "And we'll be doing a lot more of it as we try to figure out where my sister is."

My shoulders felt light. "You mean it?"

Bhavani shrugged. "Let's see what you're capable of."

Chapter 10

I *followed Bhavani down the* crooked lane, no longer wincing at every uneven patch of ground we stepped on, thanks to her sandals. The river wove its way around the little cluster of moonlit shops and homes. But we weren't walking along the river. We continued on the twisting path that was almost perpendicular to the water, watching out for any signs of danger in the dark.

As the fishy smell of the riverbank became less and less detectable, the darkened street opened up into a huge bazaar that was eerily quiet this early in the predawn morning. There were canopies whose colors I couldn't clearly see in the gloom, propped up by wooden beams attached to tall buildings. There were smaller stalls too, in the cramped market that had to have been five times the size of the one in our village.

We passed a couple pariah dogs curled up in balls next to a sleeping cow. Directly ahead I could just make out dozens of bungalows, illumined by hurricane lanterns as a few occupants here and there began to prepare for the day before the sun rose. There were homes spaced out with what seemed like large amounts of land, based on the lack of lanterns in those dark spaces, and other bungalows close together. I wondered how many of those large homes were occupied by the British and how many by Indians.

Even the smaller homes seemed to loom large over us, their windows and doors looking eerily like pained faces in what little light there was from diye, the little clay lamps shaped like bowls, and hurricane lanterns with handles.

As we neared the last of the bazaar stalls where the road dead-ended into another, I heard a baby cry, its wails carrying with the wind so early in the day when most of Indranagar was still asleep. I turned right on the perpendicular lane toward the sound, but Bhavani turned left, continuing down a path crowded with stores and smaller homes. "Bhavani!" I said, startling a sleeping cat, who meowed in the dark. "There's a baby this way."

I saw the lantern stand still. "The girl Chhaya didi watches can't be a baby," Bhavani said.

"The girl could have a baby sister or brother now. Or this could help us find another ayah who knows your Chhaya didi. Come on," I urged softly as roosters began to crow.

The light grew brighter as Bhavani returned. "It's coming from one of the bungalows."

She held the hurricane lantern up, and we could just barely make out the home to our left. It was totally dark, though, and the baby's cries weren't coming from inside this bungalow. We walked past it, Bhavani somehow getting in front of me and leading the way again even though this was my idea. She raised the lantern toward the gate of the next bungalow.

"Who goes there?" a shaky male voice asked in Hindi. In the dim light I could see the shadow of an Indian man sit up from the cot he was sleeping on outside.

Bhavani put the lantern by her face so he could see her. "I'm looking for my sister."

"It's just me and my sons in this house," the man said, lying back down.

The baby cried louder as the noisy roosters briefly quieted down.

"It's next door," Bhavani said, leading the way again.

Someone had a lantern out in the front yard. It was a skinny man in a white-and-red kurta paijama with a wide white turban on his head. He was holding the light for a British girl who looked to be ten. She was skipping around a banyan tree in a dress that looked soft enough to sleep in. The piercing sound of a baby sobbing could be heard behind her, in her bungalow.

I suddenly felt sweaty and shaky, seeing a British girl so close, wondering why she was up so early when the sun wasn't even up, wondering if we would get in trouble for talking to her.

"Where's your ayah?" Bhavani asked in Hindi.

The girl didn't look our way.

"We should go," I whispered.

Bhavani said something again. This time in English. I didn't understand everything she said, but I recognized the word *ayah*.

"I'm too old to have an ayah." The girl didn't even glance our way as she replied in perfect Hindi, without a trace of an accent. "And I've been up all night, thanks to that crying, and don't need any more disturbances," she added with a yawn, turning her back to us.

Bhavani kicked the dirt, then ran in the opposite direction of the bungalows. She passed the market to our left and headed toward the cramped homes and buildings ahead.

"Bhavani, wait!" I shouted, running after her.

I finally caught up just as we passed a couple men smoking beedis in the shadows of an alley. I heard a woman and man arguing in the darkness too, their angry words echoing. And then a dog began to howl. I shivered, hoping Bhavani wouldn't notice how scared I was, and took a couple faster steps so I could be right next to her. But I *was* scared. Terrified.

"Where are we going?" I asked Bhavani.

"Exploring," she replied angrily.

"But are there any British people living in these smaller homes?" I asked, trying to keep up with her by following the lantern light.

Bhavani suddenly stopped. Directly ahead of us, several large, brown, rectangular one-story brick buildings stood, each large enough to fit ten houses the size of my home.

"Are these homes?" I asked softly, hating how helpless I sounded.

"Don't be silly," Bhavani replied. "They're obviously barracks. The sepoys live there."

My hands felt cold and clammy. Now that she'd mentioned the sepoys, I could hear loud snores coming from inside the barracks. Sepoy Charan was probably inside one of them, back with his unit, but that didn't make me feel safer. Shadowy trees loomed on our right. To our left, a couple of Indian men ran by us, laughing and stumbling as they entered one of the crowded homes in the lanes on that side.

"So you think Chhaya is in one of those?" I asked.

Bhavani grabbed my hand and pulled me back behind a couple of mango trees across from the barracks. I followed her gaze. There, just past the barracks, was a lone red sandstone archway with a tower on either side of it, remnants of a tiny fort from long ago, before the Europeans had invaded and turned this town into a trading post. A handful of sepoys guarded the gate, their heads bobbing every now and then like they were trying to fight off sleep.

"That has to be their magazine where all the arms are stored," Bhavani whispered.

"Let's go back toward the bungalows," I whispered, unsure which was scarier, more sepoys or more people from the British East India Company. "Let's search for your sister when the sun comes up. Let's—"

But Bhavani just ran toward the sepoys, the lantern swaying. "He's inside!" she squealed.

I froze behind my tree trunk as the sepoys snapped to attention. "What? Who? And who are you?" they shouted, alarmed and startled.

"The rebel! I saw him walk by. He seemed like he was up to no good, so I followed him and saw him sneak inside when you fell asleep!"

The sepoys turned to one another. "Why weren't you watching?" one thundered.

"Why weren't *you*?" the other retorted, shoving his shoulder and opening the gate to the magazine. They ran inside to search for the rebel. Bhavani ducked in after them.

"What are you doing?" I hissed after her. This made no sense. How would entering a magazine help find Bhavani's sister?

I wanted to run away, but a part of me felt like I owed Bhavani something. After all, she had saved my life just a few hours earlier. And somehow following her seemed less scary than being outside in this town in the dark all by myself.

So I left my hiding spot and entered the magazine. Inside, to the left, stood a couple of cannons. Just past them was the windowless building Bhavani and the sepoys must have entered. I ran in after them. The air was hot and stale, and I could hear the sepoys screaming for the nonexistent rebel to show himself. To my right, Bhavani was searching the stacks of crates, peering through the gaps in the wood boxes, but she couldn't find what she was searching for.

"This is impossible." Bhavani frowned. She tilted the lantern so some of the oil spilled onto the wooden crate, causing the light to dance on its wick.

I remembered what Hari Chacha had said about the magazine blowing up in Delhi. Everything in here was flammable or worse. "Watch out!" I shouted.

That was when someone pulled both of us back.

Chapter 11

"*Stop right there!*" *a* voice shouted in heavily English-accented, strange-sounding Hindi.

I turned. A small group of British East India Company officers and Indian sepoys were standing behind us, lanterns in hand. A tall, lanky white man whose bony shoulders stood high, close to his ears, grabbed the lantern out of Bhavani's hands as more sepoys rushed forward.

The man smelled strange. Smoky, like the beedis the men in our village puffed. Ma always warned me to stay away from those men, who huddled together, smoking late at night.

"Where were you?" he thundered to the sepoys as he wiped snakelike trails of sweat off the sides of his reddening face. "Why was the gate to the magazine left unguarded? We've just gotten Delhi back, and you're this reckless?"

I thought about all the bloodshed in Delhi. About how angry the East India Company must have been with us Indians. About all the rebels they had hanged for treason.

"Sir, this girl warned us of a rebel inside," the larger sepoy sputtered nervously.

"So you believed these senseless little girls and left the magazine unguarded? After everything I told you about protecting it?" the British man asked, his blond mustache quivering.

My stomach dropped. He was angry. But was he angry at *me*? I hadn't done anything wrong. Had I?

The other sepoy quickly bowed. "Please forgive us, Captain Keene."

Maybe it was the fact that I had had nothing but a small handful of rice and lentils for dinner last night, but I suddenly felt weak. My knees shivered. My hands shook. This was Captain Keene. *The* Captain Keene. The man who was enforcing the sati laws. The man who was ordering mutineers hanged just for trying to take back their land. The man who ran the little trading post towns in this small part of India. And I was standing before him, next to boxes of cartridges and who knew what else, looking like a mutineer who was trying to destroy them.

I began to cry. "Please don't hang us," I begged. It just wasn't right. It wasn't fair. I hadn't escaped my cruel fate in the village to lose my life because of someone else—again.

The captain bent down, his gray eyes locked on mine as he spat out the Hindi words. "You're both children. Unlike your people, I do not kill children." Then he stood back up. "Vinay!" he shouted in my face as he rose before adding something else in English.

I was so scared of who Vinay was and what he was going to do, I wanted to grab Bhavani's hand for support. But I didn't think she would like that. Besides, she was calmly staring straight at Captain Keene without even a hint of perspiration.

"Vinay!" Captain Keene screamed again.

A shirtless little boy entered the magazine with a large woven fan about four times his scrawny width. It was hard to make out his face in the dark, but from his height, he seemed to be around eight years old. With a great bit of effort, he began to swing the fan from left to right, cooling the Englishman, who breathed a sigh of relief.

"That's better," Captain Keene muttered in Hindi, running his hand over the crates Bhavani had been snooping around. "Now, what to do with these two?" He glowered down at us, and even though I knew he was doing it to scare me, I shivered. "Where are their parents?" he asked, turning to the sepoys.

"We don't have any," Bhavani replied.

The man's eyelids fluttered, signaling he'd heard Bhavani, but he didn't outright acknowledge us. He just continued in Hindi, clearly meant for us to understand. "I could put them in prison for trespassing. But prison is no place for young girls."

My heart thumped hard in my chest. The corner of his lips curled up like he was enjoying scaring us.

"I could set them free, but with the rebel scum of the population prone to rioting, and dacoits and thugs outside each town, they wouldn't be safe there, either."

He was going to hang us. I knew it. It was the easiest option. The British hanged so many Indians in Delhi, many for no reason at all. He wouldn't have to worry about our well-being if we were dead.

"Yes, take them to the estate," said the captain.

"They can work off their crime of trespass there."

My hand rushed to my mouth. Had I escaped my destiny just to end up a servant for a foreign intruder?

My mind began to race. Servants were usually men and boys, except for ayahs—the nannies, like Bhavani's sister—who cared for Europeans' babies. But we were too young to be ayahs. Would we be paid? Or compensated with shelter and food? The Indian talukdars living in towns who collected tax from the farmers in our village had servants too. Some servants were paid fairly. Others worked all the time and barely got paid. What if Captain Keene hurt us?

Even if my plan was to eventually earn money, I wasn't sure I wanted this path to it. If I worked for someone in the East India Company, I could be ordered around like a sepoy. Would that be any better than if Krishna had lived and I had to listen to his family? I wasn't sure which path was better. And I wasn't sure I even had a choice in the matter anyway. Once again, my fate was being decided for me.

I wiped an anxious trickle of sweat from my forehead and glanced at Bhavani in the waning light of the lanterns as the sepoys led us away.

It was strange. Bhavani seemed to be smiling.

Chapter 12

The sepoys, with Vinay right behind them, led Bhavani and me past two guards at the iron gate side entrance of the brick wall surrounding the sprawling Keene estate. As the morning sun rose, drenching the city in pinks and oranges, we could see just how massive the captain's property was.

The sepoys paused. "Vinay will take it from here," one of them said gruffly, gesturing to the little boy. The sepoy spat onto the ground. "Make sure you listen. Captain Keene isn't someone you want to anger. He'll punish the boy if he doesn't teach you everything right."

I nodded. As the sepoys left, I put my hands on my belly and exhaled, trying to calm myself down. In the distance, near the middle of the captain's walled compound, surrounded by towering trees, was a line of crumbling old earthen shacks. They were like wilting plants, their thatch roofs tilting unevenly on one side. I frowned as Vinay paused in front of one particularly battered house with his lantern.

"This is where the servants live who don't have homes nearby," he said. "This is where you'll stay." He went inside, beckoning us to follow, then crouched by a couple rolled-up gadde a foot away from his resting lantern. The thin cotton mattresses were next to a tiny bundle of clothes that Vinay began sorting through.

But I needed to talk to Bhavani first. I bowed to the neem tree in front of the little home with a thankful namaste, then broke off a bitter twig and chewed the end until it fanned out into a toothbrush. "Why did you go in the magazine? Now look at the mess we're in."

Bhavani shrugged. "I thought this would be the fastest way to find my sister."

"How would trespassing help? How'd you know the captain would catch us?" I brandished my neem-brush at her as my voice rose in frustration. "How could you know he would make us work for him instead of hanging us, when they've hanged so many Indians, sometimes for no reason?" I lowered my voice, taking a step away from the home as Vinay appeared in the doorway. "Why aren't we running away?" I asked, brushing my teeth. "And why are you suddenly fine working for the British when you got so angry at Sepoy Charan for this just a few hours ago?"

"If you don't like what I'm doing, don't do it," Bhavani snapped. "I didn't ask you to follow me."

"Were you trying to blow the magazine up?" I asked, a little louder than I had intended.

Bhavani's eyes widened. "Just stop before the boy thinks we're up to something and reports back to Keene." She smiled at Vinay and entered the little one-room home.

But I didn't feel reassured by anything she had said. It was clear Bhavani was hiding something. I threw the neem twig down. Suddenly all the goodwill I had toward her for saving my life was gone. I took off her sandals in the doorway and handed them back to her with a frown. I wanted answers, but she didn't seem to want to give me any that were truthful.

"Maybe we're replacing an ayah who just quit, like my sister," Bhavani said with a forced smile, like we hadn't just argued. "How many children does the captain have?"

Vinay shook his head. "None."

My cheeks flushed. "See?" I turned to Vinay. "So what exactly are we doing here?" I asked, louder than I intended.

"You'll be working in the kitchen, didi," Vinay replied, using the respectful term for a big sister. Ravi used to call me that.

Vinay handed us saris he'd picked up out of the pile. They were white with navy-blue-and-gold borders and navy-blue blouses.

The fabric was faded and almost threadbare in spots, but I was eager to get out of my damp clothes, and the extra clothes in my bundle were just as damp. But I was still confused by Bhavani wanting to stay and work for a British family when she hated what they were doing to Indians—and just as confused by our job. "We're girls. Girls don't work as servants."

Vinay shrugged. "You'll get wages once a month. But rent will be deducted, so it's not a lot. You can eat leftovers from the kitchen. The captain won't let other servants do that, but we're children, so it's okay."

"And that's how I'm going to make money while

looking for my sister. Get it now, Meera?" Bhavani asked rudely, clearly still irritated by my questions.

Vinay pointed to the saris. "You'll get new clothes soon. Those were my mother's." He bit his lip like Ma did when she was sad. "She passed away last year."

Bhavani sighed as the leaky roof let some teary raindrops in. "I'm sorry."

"Me too," I said. Leaving Ma wasn't as terrible as what Vinay had gone through.

"It's okay." Vinay pointed to the faded, dirt-stained cotton quilts thrown over the earthen floor. "Those are mine and my mother's. But we can share." He smiled shyly, walking around the lantern. "I keep the light close by. Just in case the ghost on the hill comes."

The hairs on my arm stood up. Ma used to tell stories of the ghost of a servant who'd haunted her village when she was a child. The servant had drowned in the well while fetching water early one morning. On moonless nights, he could be seen walking in circles around the well, his feet backward, like all ghosts'.

The sun's rays grew brighter, making me feel less terrified. It was much easier to be afraid of ghosts in the dark.

"What about working off our crime like Captain Keene said?" I asked, stepping outside. "How much will he take each month for that?"

Vinay shrugged. "Half? He has bigger things to worry about. He just wanted to scare you so you won't go near the magazine again. You'll make up for trespassing with your work."

I waited for Bhavani to say something about how Captain Keene was the one trespassing, but instead she said, "And you'll have a roof over your head and food in your belly. You want to start over again, right? Choose your destiny and all that? You're going to need money to do that." Bhavani pointed to the pouch I had tied to the sari's drawstring. "I felt how light it was when we pulled you onto the boat. That won't be enough to buy a house or even rent one for long, especially if you want to travel far from your village to do it."

I frowned, tired of Bhavani's excuses that made no sense. "How do you know?"

"I've learned enough math in school to know that," she countered. "And I know how much my father paid to rent our little house. Didn't you learn anything in school?"

I shook my head, running my fingers over the scratches on my knuckles from the fields I had run through to escape my father. When I was six, I had tried to sit in on Babuji's class. He'd taken the stick he used on the boys' knuckles when they misbehaved and hit my knuckles instead. He'd told me an education would be wasted on me. I wasn't going to use it to solve any great problems one day. I was going to go to Krishna's house and be a good wife and then a mother. He told me I was selfish for wasting the boys' time and taking away from their education. The pain of his words, more than the actual blow, was like a jolt through the core of my bones.

After that, I only tried listening from a safe distance, from up in a tree. But it was hard to hear from there, and Ma always caught me and took me with her to cook or clean or do some other task, so I never learned much of anything, other than how to avoid upsetting Babuji.

Bhavani raised an eyebrow at me. She probably thought my situation was as strange as I found hers, where a girl was welcome to get an education and her father encouraged it. "Okay. Then see this pouch of yours? When it is full of coins, you'll have enough to buy some land." She clenched the pouch. "Assuming the bangles and necklace I can feel in there are gold."

I nodded hesitantly. Maybe it *was* a good plan to stay here with Bhavani, just for a bit, to make enough money to start over and be free to lead the life I wanted. Even if she wasn't being totally honest with me.

A few hours ago, I'd almost lost my life on someone else's fiery funeral pyre. Now I had a roof over my head. Granted, this roof would leak any time it rained, but still, dirty rainwater sounded better than a burning pyre.

🌿 🌿 🌿

Dressed in our clean saris, Bhavani and I followed Vinay past a round brick well several dozens of feet from the servants' quarters. The well was much smaller than the large stepwell back in my village, whose stairs we could walk down and whose water we could swim in, but this well wasn't meant to quench the thirst of an entire village, just Captain Keene and his family.

We headed through clusters of trees and flowering plants as male servants walked by wearing white kurta paijama with the same navy-blue-and-gold borders our saris had. One was sweeping the dusty garden paths.

Another scaled a towering palm tree to cut coconuts. His legs were wrapped around the trunk, ankles tied together, and he held fabric to lasso his way up.

Yet another man began tending to plants in the garden full of guava and fig trees, bushes of berries, fragrant eucalyptus trees, and what seemed to be flowers of every color possible. There were red hibiscuses, white jasmines; magenta bougainvillea; and wildflowers ranging from deep purples and oranges to pale pink. The garden was humming with bees. I had never seen anything like it, and I couldn't help but think of all the different color combinations of flowers I could pick for Ma's morning puja . . . until I remembered I would never be picking flowers for her again.

The captain's white bungalow was long and rectangular with columns holding the roof up. The rooftop terrace had flower pots on its border, giving the illusion that the entire top of the bungalow was covered with pastel petals and plants. A troop of monkeys jumped from coconut tree to mango tree above, causing raindrops from the night before to sprinkle down on us.

Bhavani and I followed Vinay along the veranda's outer back wall until we got to a set of five steps that led to the large stone patio. Just the veranda was three times the size of my home in the village, and it wrapped around the bungalow to join the front porch on the other side of the house. We passed a large pile of dishes waiting to be washed on the side, and a wooden stool several feet past that, and approached the back doors to the bungalow. They were surrounded by a wall of floor-to-ceiling glassless windows with bars.

A woman's voice addressed Vinay in English through the bars.

Even though the words sounded friendly, I clenched Bhavani's arm. I only recognized Vinay's name in what the woman had said and didn't know what her intentions were. The doors opened to reveal a British woman standing in the back hall of the bungalow. She passed us, heading onto the veranda as we stepped reverentially back and out of her way. She was in a long, flowing peach dress with a huge ruffled skirt that seemed like way too many layers for the hot, humid September weather. A funny-looking hat shaded her freckled face, and a few strands of her brown curls fell around her dark eyes. Strings of expensive pearls were draped around her neck, showcasing a large green emerald that would have matched Ma's favorite sari just perfectly.

Vinay repeated the woman's words back to her, like it was a greeting.

She sat down on the wooden stool, opened a little journal, and began sketching the flowers around us in great detail as we just stood frozen.

"And who do we have here?" she asked in Hindi, not lifting her eyes off her drawing.

"New servants, Memsahib," Vinay answered, using the respectful title for European women.

"What?" The woman dropped her pencil in the crease of her journal. "These little girls? When we have company coming?"

Vinay nodded. "Sahib's orders."

"*Good morning*, Memsahib." Bhavani said in English with a brusque smile, repeating the same phrase Vinay and Memsahib had used. I was shocked how confidently she spoke English yet again to a British person. She must have learned a lot in school.

"But . . . they're girls!" Memsahib said. "No one else here has native girls working for them. We're not running a charity, letting everyone stay here on our land."

Bhavani leaned into me. "Our stolen land," she corrected in a hushed whisper.

"I heard that," Memsahib said curtly in Hindi. "And if my husband wants you to work here, then that's what will happen. You're lucky we're both so generous, or you'd find yourselves out there with the rest of the natives, married off at a young age and forced to commit sati when your husband passed. Consider yourself safe and go on. I'll talk to him when he wakes."

"Ji, Memsahib," Vinay said as Memsahib stood up and walked down the veranda stairs to the garden.

"She's not saving me from anything," Bhavani said. "My family would never ask a girl or a woman to end her life because her husband died. Not many would. I mean, yours did, but . . ."

I sighed as she trailed off. I didn't know if this was the right choice for me. I didn't know what would happen behind those doors. I didn't know if the Keenes would be good employers or mean ones. I didn't know how I would choose my own fate and control my own destiny while working here or if I would be making money fast enough to make this job worthwhile. I didn't know if I was about to make a huge mistake.

I felt the weight of my dowry swinging on my waist and in that moment wished more than anything that I had a mother like that sparrow all those birthdays ago, who would have fought for me a little more. Instead, I was just a helpless hatchling all alone, with no one to fly to my defense.

Chapter 13

"*There's a lot to* do today," Vinay said as we set foot inside on the cool slate tiles of the back hall. "The collector and nawab are coming over to celebrate the end of the Delhi siege."

I nodded, trying not to get overwhelmed by all the new information. The collector collected taxes and fees from Indians for the British East India Company. Something about the idea of the British man charging Indians for our own products in our own land made me feel a little sick.

Behind the double doors, in the back hallway, was a golden birdcage housing a black koel. "That's Lal," Vinay said.

Bhavani shuddered. "Pretty unnatural, isn't it?"

"Why? Because it isn't a pet parrot like normal?" I asked, smiling as the bird, whose eyes were the same color as his name, red. He hopped in the cage, tilting his head curiously at me. A little bell tied to his foot jingled as he stomped around, pacing back and forth in the tiny cage.

"Because he isn't free," Bhavani said, shaking her head.

"That's the study," Vinay said, pointing behind the birdcage to the two faded green doors with peacocks and parrots carved in their wood directly across from the veranda doors. I imagined what they must have looked like before the color had faded. I wondered if they would have matched Ma's favorite sari. "It's where all the important documents are, so you aren't allowed in there unless Captain Keene or Memsahib tell you."

Bhavani paused in front of the closed doors, running her fingers down the sculpted birds.

To the right of the study were double doors leading to a large formal sitting room full of fancy furniture I'd never seen in our village. Vinay turned to the left and led us into the kitchen, where someone was already cooking noisily, banging metal pots and pans.

"Surely there must be other British families in this town with ayahs," said Bhavani.

"Lots." Vinay nodded. "Just not in this house." He gestured ahead. "This is Abbu," he said, using another word for *father*. "You'll be working with him in the kitchen."

In the early morning sunlight filtering in through the ber tree leaves at the corner window, Abbu smiled at us from the kitchen floor, not even batting an eye at the fact that we would be working with him. He was frail and wrinkled, his beard all white. He wore a white topi, a skull cap, like the Muslim men in my village did.

Abbu was cutting potatoes on a hasiya, the curved sickle blade attached to a wooden board. He stopped cutting and rifled through the containers behind him, making music as their contents rattled inside. "Here. Eat," he said, giving us handfuls of savory fried pastries and sliced jackfruit.

Bhavani and I began stuffing our faces with the strong-smelling, sweet yellow jackfruit. Vinay took his food with him as he headed into the dark house to start his morning duties with a couple older servants. Abbu pointed them out as they rushed in and out of various rooms. There was Dharamveer, with oily hair he kept running his fingers through, who kept staring at me and Bhavani like we didn't belong here. And Salim was a crabby-looking man with dimples in his cheeks even when he didn't smile, which it seemed like was generally the case.

Salim dropped a couple green coconuts off in the kitchen from the man who was climbing the coconut tree. Then Dharamveer and he grabbed plates from the kitchen, Dharamveer making a point to shake his head any time he spotted us. The men and Vinay headed through the far end of the kitchen to the dining room doors to the right.

A skinny white man pushed his way past me from behind. He said something brusquely in English I didn't understand. But I definitely could understand the way he shoved me out of the way with his elbows as he passed, like I was just a fly you could swat away.

"That's Cook," Abbu said in quick Hindi as Cook went to the part of the kitchen that was obstructed from our view by the open dining room doors to the right. "He doesn't speak much Hindi. He's in charge of the kitchen most of the week. But on Fridays, the captain likes to have some native food, so I am in charge. That makes Cook angry. The British don't like giving up their territory." He grinned widely, and I noticed several spots where his teeth were missing.

Cook began to rush back and forth between corners of the kitchen, grabbing utensils and picking oranges out of a bowl as he shouted about something in English.

Bhavani told me Cook was upset, which I could plainly see. Prasad, who worked in the garden, went to get more water from the well, but he hadn't brought enough coconuts for all the guests, and the captain always wanted coconut water with breakfast.

Cook dumped a tray of papayas on the floor in front of where we were sitting. I could tell he wanted them cut, so we began chopping the large fruits on smaller wooden boards, pushing the fruit over the sickles to slice them. Something squawked loudly, and I jumped, nearly cutting my finger.

"It's just Lal." Abbu chuckled. "You look like you just saw the ghost on the hill."

My ears burned with embarrassment.

"He's hungry. You can go outside and get him some—"

"Fruit!" I said triumphantly. I often spotted koels under the canopy of a ber tree back home, munching on the berries.

I stepped around Bhavani and brushed against the bark of the ber tree by the kitchen window. Something about it made me miss home, made me almost miss Babuji. The ber tree wasn't in bloom in September, but the guava tree next to it was. The fruit that had fallen to the ground was smashed. I could hear Lal cawing impatiently inside. I wasn't sure the rotten fruit would appease him so he didn't annoy Captain Keene and his guests at breakfast. I'd have to climb a tree to reach good fruit.

I grabbed the lowest branches, which were a little damp from last night's rain. Putting my left foot into a knot in the trunk, I pulled hard and boosted myself up. I crossed to another branch and pulled a handful of guavas off it. Carefully, I climbed back down the tree with just one hand, the other cradling the fruit, then jumped down and rushed back inside.

I smiled at Lal in his cage by the veranda doors and was about to feed him when I noticed the weathered emerald-green study doors were open. I looked around. No one was nearby, so I peeked inside, curious to see what was so important there that we weren't allowed near it.

I found Bhavani standing behind a large wooden desk, moving papers around. Lal let out a loud chirp, and her head snapped up with a start.

"What are you doing?" I hissed as Bhavani rushed out of the room.

"I . . . I forgot what Cook told me to do. His Hindi is so bad."

"He mostly speaks English. I thought you understood English," I replied.

"Most of it," Bhavani said. "But his accent is so hard to understand when he's yelling." She ran out of the study, closing the double doors quietly. "Oh! He asked me to put flowers on the dining room table."

I followed her to the veranda doors, but my footsteps felt heavy—like maybe I had chosen the wrong person to guide me through this new life without Ma. I may not have gone to school like Bhavani, but even without her smarts, it was obvious to me that she was lying again.

Bhavani stepped onto the veranda and took a bouquet of colorful flowers from Dharamveer, who gave her a little scowl, and I turned to Lal's birdcage.

I slid the little golden bar out of the lock, making sure my hand blocked the entrance and Lal didn't fly out. I dropped the guavas into the cage and then slid the lock back into place.

The bird hopped toward me and began to nibble at the fruit. I beamed at Lal like a mother bird.

But then I took in his obstructed view. He could see the outside world from a few feet behind the doors, but he had to crane his neck. It didn't seem right. So, being the protective mother bird my own Ma couldn't be, I moved a few stools and a wooden stick for the laundry away from the barred windows to the left of the doors, and scooted Lal's cage three feet to the side, so he was right in front of the window.

I pointed to the garden as the bird hopped excitedly. "That's where your food comes from. And hear that sound? Those are your friends, chirping away in the tree."

"Who moved the birdcage?" boomed an English-accented voice in Hindi.

I turned. Captain Keene stood behind me, his eyes puffy and red, like he hadn't slept much the night before. "Was it you?"

I tried to find my voice, but all I could do was back away from the cage, toward the veranda doorway, where I bumped into Bhavani, who was returning with the flowers.

"She thought the bird could use a better view," Bhavani said, her voice steady.

Captain Keene looked at the cage, and then at the veranda windows right in front of it. "If his cage is there," he said, opening one of the patio doors until it almost hit the cage, "the door would knock him over."

I looked down.

"We went through a lot of trouble to catch that bird. Next time you want to move something in my house, you ask my permission," Captain Keene said, moving the birdcage back to its original spot. Then he walked away through the ornate doors to the formal sitting room.

"Like *you* asked permission before moving things around in our land," Bhavani muttered.

I paused, waiting for my heartbeat to calm down. But it was showing no signs of slowing. I supposed it shouldn't have come as a shock. I thought about all the times I had been scared this week: scared of the marching sepoys, scared of having to live with Krishna, scared of having to live with Sheela, scared of having to leave Ma, scared of Babuji's anger, scared of sati, scared of the ghost on the hill, scared of the captain.

Cook thundered out of the kitchen, Abbu behind him. "You." He pointed at me as he sputtered in Hindi. "I saw you climb that tree. Go out and get me two coconuts. Now!"

I looked out the veranda windows at the looming coconut trees. I guessed Cook didn't know that having courage wasn't exactly something I was known for.

Chapter 14

*A*bbu rested his frail hands on the veranda wall as I stood meekly before the coconut tree in the garden. The skinny man who'd climbed the coconut tree earlier was nowhere in sight. The rope he'd used to bind his ankles together and the scarf he'd looped around the trunk were resting by the foot of the tree, along with a small sickle. "I don't know how to do this," I said shakily, as a monkey swung overhead to a neighboring mango tree.

Cook angrily shouted to me through the kitchen window, his hand gestures demanding I go up the tree.

"You can learn," Abbu said.

I pushed my finger hard into the rough bark of the palm tree, imagining how shocked I would have been if Babuji had ever told me that. A tan-and-white Rampur Greyhound on a leash dragged an Indian servant past me. The servant's white-and-red kurta paijama was different from the uniforms of the servants who worked here, and I assumed the dog and he came with the collector or nawab, who must have just arrived.

"Make sure you tie that tight around your ankles," Abbu added, pointing to the rope by the base of the tree. "That way, even if your feet get tired, they're still gripping the tree."

Sick of always being afraid, I quickly tucked my pallu into my waistband and pulled the sari up so my legs could move more freely. I sat on the damp ground, wrapped my feet around the tree trunk, and slid the rope around my legs, tying it into a tight loop around my ankles. I held the sickle with my right hand and looped the cotton cloth around the tree trunk like I had seen Prasad and countless others do when I was growing up. My palms grew sweaty, so I wiped them on my hips. The trunk was narrow, but there were grooves in it.

I took a breath, reminding myself it was just like climbing the tree in our front yard back home, and folded my legs like a frog. I pushed off with my feet on the trunk, scooting up, the rough bark scratching at my legs. When I tried to move the scarf up higher, it was a little slippery on the wet bark. I began to shake, thinking how if I fell on the sickle, it would be the end of me.

"You can do this," said Abbu. "Believe in yourself. I do."

I exhaled and willed my arms to push the cloth loop up. It worked! I did it again, breathing deeply, pushing my feet on the tree trunk and pulling myself up higher with my hands. Higher, higher, and higher, until I reached the top of the tree, where the green coconuts were.

Abbu cheered. I turned back to see his beaming face. "Now cut it at the top," he shouted.

I was about to turn back to the coconuts when I noticed Memsahib sitting in the garden below. She was sketching away, glancing over in my direction every now and then.

"Go on, Meera beti," urged Abbu, calling me "daughter" in Hindi. "Cut it."

I wrapped my left arm around the tree and sliced off a couple green coconuts with my right. They fell to the ground with a thud. My heart raced, glad the coconuts had fallen and not me.

"You did it!" exclaimed Abbu. He clapped as I scooted down the tree until I was low enough to place my feet on the earth and let go of the fabric lifeline.

I bent down, untied the rope around my ankles, straightened out my sari, and scooped up the heavy green coconuts—the reward for my bravery. But the expression on Abbu's face would have been reward enough. He was smiling from ear to ear, eyes twinkling like a proud father. Or, at least, I imagined that was how Babuji would have looked, had I ever done anything to make him proud back in our village.

❧ ❧ ❧

With the coconut water ready for breakfast, Cook practically shoved Bhavani and me into the dining room, a tray of papaya in Bhavani's hands and a tray of double roti and maakhan, or *bread and butter* as Cook had called it, in mine.

In front of me, Vinay was fanning Captain Keene, who sat at the head of the table before a large plate of eggs. We reached around him and set the trays and vase down on the long table. Dharamveer and Salim poured chai into everyone's teacups. When they stood back to wait for their next job, Bhavani followed their lead, and I followed hers.

"Delhi is finally safe and back in the hands of its rightful owner," Captain Keene announced.

Bhavani, scowling almost as much as Salim normally did, translated under her breath for me.

To the captain's left, Memsahib smiled, her face flushed from the morning sun. Beside her sat an Indian man who wasn't smiling. In fact, he seemed as upset by the captain's words as Bhavani was. He wore a deep purple turban accented with a peacock feather, an orange silk kurta adorned with embroidered flowers, and a string of pearls and dazzling gemstones around his neck. The heavy gold rings in his ear shimmered in the ray of sunlight from the windows behind him.

My eyes widened. This had to be the nawab, the governor of a territory, just like the one who used to fly a kite full of gold. Maybe he was even the nawab who ruled over all the land our villages were on, whose grandfather's birthday we celebrated. I tried not to stare.

On the other side of the captain was a red-headed man with a cane, who must have been the town's collector, and his blonde wife and yawning daughter.

I raised an eyebrow at Bhavani. It was the same girl whose house we had gone to before the sun was up.

The collector said something, raising his teacup and almost knocking over the flowers Bhavani had placed on the table.

The turbaned servant in red and white entered the dining room from the kitchen side with the dog on its leash. The dog wagged her tail and sat next to the young girl.

I couldn't help but smile. The dog made me think of the scrawny tan pariah dog with a dark brown snout that had once followed Radha Chachi home from the market. Babuji had tried shooing him away, but the dog wouldn't leave. Radha Chachi had felt so sorry for him, with his one chewed-up ear, she let him stay in our yard and named him Munna. He didn't live long, and Babuji disapproved for the full few short months he was with us, of course, but after everyone had eaten, Chachi would sneak the leftovers off to Munna. The poor mutt was so grateful for the scraps that other people had discarded that he would gobble them up, his tail wagging so hard it felt like a slap if you stood too close to him.

Cook entered a moment later, triumphantly holding a tray with six tall glasses of murky coconut water, as if he had climbed up the tree and felled the coconuts himself.

"We're so pleased you could join us," Memsahib said in Hindi to the nawab. "It's such a relief from our usual company. And the usual *company's* company talk." She smiled at her wordplay, which Bhavani had to explain to me because I didn't know the English word *company*.

"Yes, Nell is quite bored with all the talk of taxes, business, shipments, and strategy over meals," the captain added as Bhavani softly interpreted for me. *"I tell her all the time not to pay it any heed. You'll just get bogged down by it, dear."* He patted his mouth and offered Memsahib a smile before turning to the nawab. *"After all, it's men's work. She should stick to her drawings."*

Memsahib smiled politely and looked down. I studied her face as a hint of a blush spread over her ears. It was strange. The British Empire had a queen, just like Jhansi had a rani. A female ruler. Yet Memsahib was being told what she was allowed to do by a man. Just like Babuji told me what I could do, and Krishna would have told me, had he lived.

The collector tapped his finger on the shiny plate before him, making a jittery clink. *"I should add it's a good thing we men are doing so much work around here, protecting women. Stopping all these awful, backward customs like sati. Right, Nawab?"*

"Sati is awful and backward," the nawab replied in Hindi, spreading his cloth napkin on his lap. "As were the Salem Witch Trials in America and what the British did to women they accused of witchcraft here. As was the way women were burned at the stake as punishment for certain crimes in Great Britain, when husbands could commit the same crime and not receive that awful sentence. It doesn't matter where one lives; women are rarely treated the way they should be." The nawab took a bite of his food. "As equals."

He turned to Memsahib as the collector choked on his water. "I'm sorry my wife couldn't join us," the nawab continued. "She's been so busy starting the all-girls school she was telling you about last time." He paused. "I remember how fond Franny was of the idea. She even said she wanted to teach there when she grew up."

At the mention of the name "Franny," Memsahib's mouth hung open like the words she wanted to say were lost. She turned to her husband, who quickly spoke up, gesturing toward the collector's daughter.

"This young lady here has a possible future as a teacher. Victoria was telling me earlier she has been studying really hard."

Victoria nodded, her yellow ringlets bouncing up and down. *"Reading, writing . . . I'm even working on a story right now. Just like Mother,"* she added, smiling at the collector's wife.

"Just like half the memsahibs in this land, eh?" asked her father, elbowing the captain, who rubbed his arm, annoyed.

"But I don't think teaching the native children is a job for me," Victoria said in near-perfect Hindi, eyeing me and Bhavani off in our corner of the dining room as Bhavani continued to interpret their conversation low enough that they shouldn't have heard her. "It's probably a better job for a native teacher, don't you think?" She scratched her dog under its chin.

"But your Hindi is so good," the nawab said, sipping his coconut water and turning to the adults at the table. "Her accent is better than any of yours."

"Her ayah taught her," replied the collector in Hindi so heavily accented I could just barely make out what he was saying. "Just like she's teaching William now. One has to know how to communicate with the natives."

"Raised by an Indian woman." The nawab's cheekbones ballooned as he clearly tried not to smile. "No wonder she's so smart. You have a lot more in common with these little native girls here than you might think," he added, pointing to me and Bhavani.

As Victoria scowled, I immediately looked down and walked swiftly out of the dining room. Her dog barked at my sudden movement as I ducked back into the kitchen. Bhavani followed me.

Cook, still frazzled, was in the process of dumping a pile of dirty cookware into Abbu's hands for washing. He pointed to the platters of fruit Bhavani and I had chopped earlier.

We each picked up a tray and entered the room again as the collector's wife was speaking. *"Our ayah gives me the time to finish my writing. I've already had one book published back home, you know,"* she said curtly. *"And I'll have another one done before William is two. Our stories are the only way for everyone there to know what it's like to be here, to suffer the strange music, to deal with the heat and rain and disease, to hassle with cunning servants . . . to live amongst the natives."*

I began to serve fruit to the side of the table

Memsahib was on, feeling too scared to go near the collector. Bhavani served him, who fanned a few fruit flies away from his cup and then translated what the collector's wife had said as we stepped back from the table to the wall.

"So many bugs these days," the collector muttered. *"Swarms of them. Reminds me of when we used to go on those awful parades back when I was an officer. Except in addition to swarms of bugs and swarms of rebel scum, we had swarms of naked little bronze children in every town we passed through."* He turned to the nawab, raising his cane. *"I served before the injury. And now I serve as the collector. I'm not sure in which capacity I am feared more!"* He laughed once again at his own joke as the nawab gave him a polite smile.

The collector wiped a tear from his eye and continued. *"The things that happened on those marches. One lady was starving and couldn't afford to take care of her boy. I bought the little guy for a few coins, and when he was old enough, he fanned me."*

The color drained from Memsahib's cheeks. I turned to Bhavani, who quickly whispered a translation. I was pretty sure some of the color drained from my cheeks too, once she was done explaining.

"Oh, don't look at me like that," the collector said gently to Memsahib. *"Once we were marching back home a couple years later, I let him go. He must have been reunited with that vulgar woman. And if not, serves her right. Bugs. All of them. Did you know I found a large black ant floating in my teacup yesterday? Dead."*

The collector switched to bad Hindi. "At first I thought it was one of those cloves these people"—he gestured to Salim and Dharamveer, like they were one and the same, and so were all the people in our land—"like to put in everything."

The mention of the spice made me immediately think of Krishna. And the pyre. And my escape. My hand trembled a little, causing the tray I was holding to rattle.

"I couldn't believe it," the collector continued in English. Bhavani quickly whispered the translation in my ear. In that moment, the cries of a baby floated in from the sitting room behind the doors at the far end of the dining room.

"Neither could the servant, dear," said the collector's wife as a tall, skinny Indian woman in a white sari with a gold border and a red blouse walked in. Bhavani finished translating as the ayah apologetically carried

in a chubby white baby with blond ringlets. He pawed at the ayah's face, turning pinker with each cry.

"William!" The collector's wife stood to take the baby, her eyes scanning all the servants listening to the conversation. "He had the poor man flogged," she said in thickly accented Hindi, as if trying to make a point in front of all of us about how kind she was to be appalled that an Indian servant was beaten by the collector.

"Flogged?" Memsahib dabbed at her forehead with a handkerchief as Bhavani again softly interpreted from our spot by the wall. *"Because an ant crawled into your tea and drowned? Richard, you can't expect the natives to look at you with anything other than hatred when you treat them like dirty dogs."*

The ayah turned toward the collector with a defiant glare, and, seeing her face fully for the first time, Bhavani dropped the empty tray she was holding, which rattled loudly as it hit the floor. The ayah gasped, rushing to help her, but before she could reach Bhavani, Cook opened the door and dragged Bhavani into the kitchen. And I finally caught a glimpse of the ayah's round, moonlike face. My mouth dropped.

This had to be Bhavani's sister.

"Not dirty dogs, Nell," the collector replied, pointing to Victoria's pet. "Obedient dogs."

The nawab shook his head, a fire burning in his eyes as the collector laughed at another one of his own jokes.

Victoria held on to the double roti with the tips of three fingers and delicately nibbled at it. *It must take her hours to eat like this*, I thought as I stared. The girl frowned at me, saying something in English to her father that caused Memsahib to loudly clear her throat.

"Cook!" she called, motioning toward me with her eyes.

From behind me, Cook yanked me back into the kitchen by my elbow and pointed to the ground where Bhavani was sitting, her eyes shiny. "Sit," he said. "And eat."

I sat next to Bhavani. "Is that . . . your sister?" I whispered.

"I *said*, sit and eat!" Cook commanded.

Bhavani nodded at me, and I quickly looked down, chewing away like Cook had ordered. I was pretty sure I wasn't eating as daintily as Victoria. In fact, I was certain I was acting a lot more like Munna than I had realized: sitting on command, eating the leftover scraps of the British . . . just like an obedient dog.

Chapter 15

That night, after Memsahib had dismissed us for the evening with new, bright white saris with gold-and-navy-blue borders and sandals to wear tomorrow, I went with Bhavani to the collector's bungalow to find her sister, Chhaya.

Chhaya stood by the front gate to the collector's property, pushing baby William asleep in a stroller, as Bhavani and I stood on the other side of the gate by the road. "Victoria was telling the truth. Sort of," Chhaya said, her voice a slightly deeper version of Bhavani's. "I'm not her ayah anymore. I'm William's."

"Doesn't mean I trust her," Bhavani said, gripping the iron bars tightly. "Or any of them."

At the sound of a squeaking door, Chhaya looked behind her. Victoria had exited the bungalow to play with a little wooden bird on the porch. I watched as she raised her arm and ran back and forth, making the bird fly.

"You're right not to trust them," Chhaya said, her voice dropping to a whisper. "You're right to blame them for Babuji's death." Her eyes pooled with tears. "I never would have left if I knew it was the last time I'd see him."

Bhavani reached through the bars and squeezed her sister's hand.

Not wanting to intrude on the family moment, I touched Bhavani's shoulder. "I'll see you back home," I said softly, putting my hands in a namaste to bid Chhaya good-bye.

It was funny Bhavani had brought up trust. I didn't like that she was lying to me about whatever she was up to, sneaking around the study, but I was happy she had found her sister. I guessed that meant she would continue working for the Keenes until Chhaya was no longer needed as an ayah and they could buy or rent someplace with the money they saved.

I ran up the path that led to the sepoys' part of

town, turning right into the side gate of the Keenes' brick wall way before I was anywhere close to the barracks or magazine. The guards let me in, and I ran through the trees to our quarters, ducking inside. I assumed I wouldn't be seeing Bhavani that often at night, now that she had found her sister. I would have to stick with Vinay to show me around if I needed it.

He was curled up on one side of the gadde he had pushed together for us, next to his lamp that he was certain warded off the ghosts. His knees were tucked up to his chest like he was trying to hide, but there was no cot in this home to hide under. He was uttering parts of a prayer in his sleep, hands together.

Poor kid, I thought, remembering the nightmares I'd had after Ravi had died. But Ma was always there to comfort me by patting my head rhythmically until I fell back asleep. Vinay didn't have a mother to soothe him, so I knelt by his side and put my hand on his head.

Vinay's eyes were squeezed shut as he spoke in his sleep. "Franny is dead . . ."

"Who's Franny?" I asked, thinking of the ghost on the hill.

But Vinay was now moaning worse than before, mumbling, "No, Ma. Please don't die."

I patted his head, catching a glimpse of the remnants of the faded mehendi design Ma had made on my palms. I smoothed down his hair like she would do to me. One, two, three strokes . . .

The wrinkles on Vinay's forehead disappeared. His knees unlocked, and he brought his legs down. And soon his breathing became deep and slow as his nightmare ended.

Yawning, I scooted over, ready to sleep myself, when I heard laughter outside. Curious, I stepped outside. A few homes down, Prasad, Dharamveer, and others were playing a game of dice by a flickering lamp.

Prasad caught my eye and then proceeded to roll his. "What are you staring at? You should be an ayah caring for a baby, not cooking for the British like you're one of the men."

A bunch of the men laughed again, but one stood up and walked toward me. "It's okay, Meera," he said weakly. It was Abbu. "Wait right there." He ducked into his abode.

I waited as Prasad gave me one last nasty look before returning to his game. Finally, Abbu emerged with a wad of fabric in his hands. He led me back inside my little home. He sat by Vinay's little light, and I joined him as he shook open the scrunched-up cloth.

Six cowrie shells fell out of the material, along with twelve wooden mounds, the playing pieces. Four were yellow with a black border, four were black with a yellow border, four were red with a green border, and four were green with a red border.

Abbu spread the cloth out on the ground. It was a two-foot-by-two-foot cross-shaped piece of embroidered cotton. There was a colorful star sewn into the center of the cross, and the four arms of the cross had several different colored squares, like a stretched-out chess board. I recognized the game. It was pachisi. I had seen Ma and some of her friends playing it before.

Abbu gave me four yellow and four black pieces and handed me the six shells. "Roll."

I shook the shiny shells. They rattled against one another, and then I dropped them to the ground. Four of them were mouth-side up, the jagged opening in the shell smiling up at me. I moved a wooden piece four squares counterclockwise, up one arm of the cross.

I glanced over at Vinay, who was now sound asleep, his eyebrows level. "Abbu? Who's Franny?"

Abbu's hand froze mid-roll. "Who told you about Franny?"

I pointed to Vinay. "I think he's having nightmares about his mother dying after Franny."

Abbu nodded over and over as he played. "Yes, I suppose he would."

"Why?" I asked, shaking the shells for my turn.

"Franny was the captain's daughter."

I dropped the shells earlier than I had intended. "Memsahib had a child?"

"A wonderful child," Abbu replied, taking his turn. "Vinay's mother was her ayah. But Franny got sick and passed away, and an hour later, so did Vinay's mother." Abbu quickly changed the subject. "You know, you remind me of my own daughter. She was so smart when she was little, no one could beat her at pachisi."

"What happened to her?" I asked, afraid it would be yet another death story.

But Abbu beamed, rolling the shells and moving his pieces. "Fatima got married when she was young. Money was tight with her dowry. So I joined the sepoys. Head cook. That's how I met Captain Keene. I haven't seen Fatima in ages. But we exchange letters at Eid."

I shook the shells in my hand for an extra-long time. I didn't know any girls who could read and write other than Bhavani. I thought about how Babuji never taught me much of anything, other than to fear him, and released the handful. Three shells smiled at me, so I moved my piece three squares forward, landing on Abbu's red-and-green piece, capturing it.

"Ack!" squeaked Abbu, putting his hands around his neck, sticking his tongue out, and rolling his eyes back into his head as he keeled over to the ground.

Unable to control myself, I giggled loudly. Abbu chuckled, the gaps in his teeth showing until his laugh dissolved into a noisy cough he tried to muffle in his shoulder.

Vinay turned in his sleep, frowning.

Abbu put his finger to his lips, and in the dim light, I could see a blotch of red on his shoulder where he had coughed. He noticed my concerned look. "It happens from time to time." He smiled. "Anyway, that's enough for tonight."

I nodded, helping Abbu clean up the game.

"Good night, Meera beti." He patted me on the head and walked out.

"Good night," I whispered, smiling as I nestled

into the thin gadda on the ground. With Ma so far away and Bhavani now busy with her sister, it felt nice to have someone care for me again. I closed my eyes on my thirteenth birthday, grateful I wasn't at Krishna's house, and even more thankful I hadn't lost my life on his pyre.

Finally feeling a little peaceful for the first time in days, I went to sleep in my new home.

October 1857

Chapter 16

Dozens of clay lamps lit up several of the servants' quarters for Diwali. An entire month had passed since Bhavani and I had started working for the Keenes, and the indigo pouch was now slightly heavier, thanks to the few coins I had earned over the weeks. In the little moments between our jobs, Bhavani had even shown me how to add the coins together and taught me how much I should plan on earning and saving each month to be able to afford food once I finally lived in my new house. I wasn't totally in control of my fate like I wanted to be, but I was earning money to get there one day. And I was safe in my routine, which was a lot like it had been back home with Ma— just minus Ma.

Every day we helped clean the house, wash dishes, cook meals while Cook snapped at us, serve the meals, feed Lal, sew buttons back on clothes, and wash and hang laundry—and on Fridays, we helped Abbu make Indian food for Captain Keene and Memsahib. And every night, when we were finally done, Bhavani would go off to spend time with Chhaya. She never invited me, and on several occasions, she would come home after I was already asleep.

This morning, Bhavani wasn't even in our home when I woke up. Had she left in the night with Chhaya? I took a deep breath of the cooler October morning air and walked with Vinay toward Captain Keene's bungalow, passing an intricate geometric rangoli design on the ground outside one of the little homes in the servants' quarters. The rangoli was made of the colorful powder of dried flowers and herbs.

As we entered the Keenes' property, passing through their garden and entering the back veranda, I smiled, remembering how much Ma loved Diwali.

I picked some fresh-looking guavas off the ground for Lal as I thought about how Ma would dress up in her most beautiful emerald-green sari and wear her gold necklace next to her mangalsutra during the holiday. I would gather flowers and fill the clay lamps with oil, soaking their cotton wicks so they could stay lit all night. Ma would crouch down by our front door to make a beautiful rangoli pattern in our doorway, along with a swastik out of white powder. The cross with four arms bent was the ancient Hindu symbol of auspiciousness, a good omen. Babuji would always pause in the front yard to take in our creations before mentioning the Diwali sweets and treats he was craving, like a not-so-subtle hint of what he wanted us to make the next day. It wasn't an order—it was a request—but one I always followed.

My smile faded as I realized that even though I had traveled down the river, farther than I'd ever been from home, I was still taking orders from someone else. Not much had changed.

I passed Abbu washing dishes on the veranda and was quickly snapped out of my thoughts as Bhavani bounded toward me from inside the house.

"You're already here?" I asked, scrunching up my brow as I entered the bungalow with Vinay, who waved at Bhavani before turning into the kitchen to begin his work. I gently opened Lal's cage to give the bird the guavas, making sure he didn't fly out.

"I was up almost all night," she replied, practically bouncing on her feet, full of energy despite not sleeping much.

"Chhaya didi introduced me to so many new friends. We all think alike. We all want the same thing."

I watched Lal peck at the soft flesh of the fruit, tearing into it. Bhavani seemed to like these new friends much better than me.

"A roof over their head and food in their bellies?" I asked.

Bhavani crossed her arms, confused.

"Is that what you and your new friends want? Like you and I do?" I asked, trying to remind Bhavani of what she had said the night we came to this property, trying to make her remember that I was her friend too so she wouldn't just forget about me and leave me here all by myself. Even if she was a liar, I didn't want to be in this house without her. Something about Bhavani made me feel safe.

Bhavani walked over to the green double doors engraved with parrots and peacocks and began to wipe the dust off. When the doors creaked open from the force of her wiping, she raised an eyebrow at me and stepped into the study to wipe the back side of the doors.

"You're not allowed to do that!" I whispered urgently to Bhavani, clenching the sari pallu draped over my head, hoping Captain Keene or Memsahib wouldn't catch her.

Bhavani took a step back into the hall. "That's what I thought."

"What?" I asked, a hot, annoyed flush sweeping through my cheeks.

Abbu walked by us with a tower of dried dishes from the veranda. The back doors swung open and shut behind him as he passed Lal's cage and entered the kitchen.

"My friends and I are a little different than you," Bhavani replied once Abbu was out of earshot. "We wouldn't get upset if one of us entered Captain Keene's study."

"But you're not supposed to go there," I replied, grabbing the broom leaning against the wall. I bent down and swept at the floor, kicking up a small cloud of dust. "Captain Keene and Memsahib don't want you to."

"What gives them the right to say where we can and cannot go?" Bhavani bit her lower lip so hard I was afraid it was going to start bleeding. She stepped around me, dusting Lal's cage as he happily gobbled up the last of the sweet fruit. "What gives them the right to come into our land and hurt us to make themselves rich?"

She swiped extra hard at the birdcage, and it wobbled a little on the stool.

"Stop," I cried. "You'll hurt him."

"Hurt him? *They* hurt him. They've caged up someone that deserves to be free, just so he can sing for them."

"Indian people keep birds in birdcages too," I replied, remembering a traveling merchant's caged parrots I once saw at our village market and how sad I felt for them, squeezed together in a cage, their vivid green feathers smashed up against one another.

"Well, they're wrong too," Bhavani said, wiping the little handle that kept the birdcage locked. "Everyone deserves freedom." She slid the handle to the left, opening the birdcage.

Unlike when I did it to feed Lal, though, her hand wasn't blocking the doorway.

"What are you doing?" I screamed, rushing toward the birdcage.

But my sudden movement startled Lal, and with a hop and a start and a jingle of the little bell tied to his foot, he flew out of the birdcage and straight out the open back doors.

Chapter 17

The sitting room's doors swung open as Memsahib rushed into the back hall. "What's all this scream-ing about?" she asked sharply. "I haven't even had my breakfast—" She stopped, staring at the empty birdcage. "Foolish girls! That was—that was Franny's bird!"

The loud chirp of a koel sounded, and I spotted Lal sitting on the tall veranda wall outside. Memsahib's eyes filled with tears.

I grabbed the birdcage and rushed out the door. "I'll get him!"

"Meera, wait!" Bhavani said, chasing after me.

I didn't wait, though. I was tired of listening to Bhavani when she didn't seem worthy of my admiration at all. She wasn't someone I should have felt safe with. She lied. She'd made Lal leave.

I approached Lal with the birdcage and made a soft puckering noise with my lips to get his attention. He turned toward me. I smiled, taking a step forward, and he flew off, above my head, through the trees.

"Lal!" I shouted, heading through the garden, Bhavani right behind me.

He was flying low and then sometimes high, like he was getting used to the fact that he was finally no longer in the tiny birdcage. A part of me wondered if he really were better off out in the wide world where he could spread his wings, but I would miss seeing him brighten up my mornings and hearing his song.

My arm was getting sore from holding the heavy birdcage, but I kept after the koel. Lal flew over the garden, looping past the well and the servant quarters, and over the brick wall. I raced after him as the guards let me out the side gate, and Bhavani caught up to me.

"Look how happy he is," she panted as we turned left down the path, following the bird toward the bazaar. "Unlike the poor weavers and artisans in Indranagar, robbed out of fair payment for their creations."

"There are hawks out here," I snapped, turning to the right. We passed stalls selling muslin, silk, cotton, and chintz in a stunning array of jewel tones; shops selling woven fabrics and sculpted art; and folk jewelry made out of silver-colored metals. I swallowed, thinking of the weavers in Bhavani's village who'd cut off their thumbs to be free of the British. "And Lal probably doesn't know how to find food on his own. He could die out here without us taking care of him."

"You sound just like Memsahib," Bhavani said, as Lal hopped down the colorful fabric canopies of the stalls, going from merchant to merchant.

I struggled to keep up, craning my neck up and almost bumping into several merchants who were wishing one another a happy Diwali and a prosperous new year.

Bhavani followed. "Tricking yourself into thinking you're saving someone by caging them and making them dependent on you for everything, when all you really want is to steal his song and keep it for yourself. Well, his song isn't yours to keep."

Lal chirped loudly from the canopy of a fancy jewelry shop where a crowd had gathered to purchase

Diwali gifts. I ducked under multiple people's arms to get to him. As I got closer, I saw an arm with real gold bangles with elephants carved on them.

As Lal flickered his tail feathers above, I couldn't shake the feeling that I had seen those bangles before. I took a breath and lifted the birdcage, trying not to hit anyone in the crowd, and made the puckering noise at Lal.

"How much are those?" a girl's voice shouted over me from ahead. She turned to the side as Lal's bell jingled right above me. My hand began to shake at the sight of her face.

It was Sheela. She was standing right in front of Krishna's brother. This was Sheela's jeweler. I had known Indranagar was her hometown, but I never thought I'd ever run into her here, when she now lived in Krishna's home so many villages away.

I lowered the birdcage with my trembling arm, and Lal flew off high into the air, until the sound of his jingling bell could no longer be heard.

Tears slipped down my cheeks, and my heart raced as Sheela turned back to say something to Krishna's brother. I felt hot, like I was next to Krishna's funeral pyre. Sweating, I backed into the crowd, ducking down, fighting my way back out to the path where Bhavani was.

I grabbed her arm, squeezing it. "He's gone," I said, my voice wavering with panic at the thought of how disappointed Memsahib would be to know we'd lost her bird forever. And at the fear that Sheela might turn around and catch me.

"Let's go." I led her down the path, away from the market, thinking about how I wouldn't hear Lal tomorrow morning when I entered the bungalow. I wouldn't see his beak almost smiling as he gobbled up the fruit I would collect for him. I'd never see my friend again.

I rubbed my running nose on the shoulder of my blouse and reminded myself I shouldn't be sad. I was being sad for selfish reasons. Lal was a wild animal. He deserved to be outside, gathering his own fruit, flying freely, tasting the wind as he soared through the air.

I wiped my tears away and turned to Bhavani. "Maybe he *is* better off being free."

Chapter 18

"*Do you really believe* that?" Bhavani asked me as we left the market far behind and I eased my grip on her arm.

Obviously I wasn't happy Lal was gone. I loved hearing him squawk and chirp and sing in the bungalow. But I just shrugged, trying to swallow down the lump forming in my throat.

Bhavani nodded, turning down the street that led to the side entrance to the Keenes'. Far off in the distance, through a thick forest, I could see the spooky old abandoned bungalow that sat at the top of the hill in the back of Captain Keene's land. What little I could make out of its windows and door through the overgrown bushes and surrounding trees looked like a terrifying face with the windows as its eyes and the door as its gaping mouth.

We passed more clay Diwali lamps outside of some small homes, and families and friends laughing and singing and dancing together as they celebrated the holiday. In contrast to their beaming faces, a group of scrawny shirtless men, ribs sticking out, huddled on the ground, their eyes hollow, their faces grim. A few were standing with baskets on their heads. Some of them were chewing paan, betel leaf stuffed with shredded betel nut, lime paste, and catechu paste.

"Laborers," Bhavani said, "waiting to see who has work for them. They built many of the roads here but were barely paid enough to feed themselves, let alone their families." One of the men loudly spat a stream of dirty crimson saliva, just missing my white sari. "Those poor men," she added.

"Poor *men*?" I asked, repulsed, making sure none of the red had splattered on me.

"My cousins were laborers in our village. It isn't easy work in the hot sun. When I first left home to find Chhaya didi, I had to travel through the big town near us," said Bhavani. "I saw a large lizard that had gotten pinned between a fallen tree and the ground. A bunch of townspeople worked together to pull the tree off it."

I breathed easier. "That's a relief."

Bhavani shook her head. "They freed it so they could eat it."

I felt ill. "That's disgusting," I said.

"If you knew what it was like to go hungry, you wouldn't say that."

We neared the sepoy barracks and the sandstone remnants of the small fort that was now the magazine that Captain Keene had caught us in. It was guarded by more sepoys than the night we had entered it, probably *because* we had entered it. A young man who looked around nineteen, with a basket of fruit on his head, was walking around the magazine, eyeing it. As he made his way past the entrance and back onto the path toward us and the crowded street, he paused in front of Bhavani and handed her a guava.

"Guavas?" he asked, the basket's shadow obstructing his eyes. But I could still see his nostrils on his pointy nose flaring.

Bhavani handed him a coin, but he shook his head, lowering the basket so its shadow was gone and we could see his gray eyes. "I'm Javed, Chhaya's friend." He handed her the guava. "We met the other day.

Were you able to find the fruit you were looking for?" he asked, almost like he was talking in code.

There was a flash of realization in Bhavani's eyes. She shook her head.

The curled ends of Javed's mustache bobbed as his frame slumped a little at her response. He nodded at me. "Is she Chhaya's friend too?"

Bhavani shook her head.

"I hope you can find that fruit. Soon," Javed said. He continued on his way, the basket back on his head.

"What was that all about?" I asked as Bhavani led us away from the magazine, back down the path, closer to the barracks.

She handed the tiny guava to a little boy on the street, whose face was coated in grime. "There's a terrible famine in so many different towns, all because the British robbed us of our place in the world. They changed us from one of the richest lands, a land that created beautiful things other countries bought, to a ravaged one full of famished people. People with ribs jutting out of their chests, people with their bellies sunken in, people so hungry their breast milk has dried up and their babies are too weak to even cry, let alone suckle, as they silently die. People whose only job is to make and grow things for the British to move forward."

Bhavani's voice rose. "Millions of Indians are starving to death while the British are shipping millions of pounds of the rice and grains we are growing to the United Kingdom. And it's all because the British don't think of us as their equals. They don't even think of us as humans. If they did, why would they let any of this happen?"

Her eyes grew glassy as she wiped at them. "You think you know about life just because you escaped death once? Thanks to the East India Company, our people, no matter what their background, no matter what religion, have to escape death daily."

I looked back. A young man with a thick beard and a dark blue turban stood behind us, staring at the entrance of the magazine. He turned to leave and almost ran into us.

"Sorry," he said, taking a step back to let us pass. But then he saw Bhavani's face and raised an eyebrow at her.

Bhavani's gaze darted to the left and right, and when it seemed like she thought it was safe to answer, she shook her head.

The man's shoulders slumped, and he walked away from us.

"Okay, what is going on?" I asked.

"With what?"

"You shook your head at that man. Who is he? Is he one of your sister's friends too? Does he have a really important question about fruit for you too?"

A group of sepoys began to laugh loudly outside the barracks, leaning against the brown brick rectangular building. I noticed one in the middle of the group. It was Sepoy Charan.

His eyes widened with surprise. He strode over to me and Bhavani. "Why did you bring her here? I told you not to involve her," he said to Bhavani softly, but I still heard.

"Not to involve me in what?" I asked loudly.

Bhavani and Charan exchanged a look and pulled me to the side, away from the other sepoys and closer to the revelers walking by on the street.

As a group of kids sang and clapped in a circle while a little girl danced in the middle of them, Bhavani sighed. "Okay. I'll tell you. But you cannot tell Memsahib or Captain Keene. Or anyone, really. See, finding my sister was just part of it," she whispered right into my ear. Her breath tickled me, but I didn't feel like laughing. "I've joined the rebellion."

My feet felt weak as I dug them into the path, trying to steady myself. "But you're . . . just—"

"What? A girl?" Bhavani asked.

My shoulders slumped.

"I tried to find the cartridges that first night in the magazine but couldn't. But now I have a plan. See, you're right. I *am* just a girl. Just a girl with access to Captain Keene's study. A girl as brave as the rani of Jhansi."

"And what about you?" I said softly to Sepoy Charan. "They'll hang you for treason if you get caught."

He shook his head. "I'm not planning on getting caught. I've been a part of the resistance since the mutiny in spring. I purposely got separated from the sepoys I was with and was meeting with other rebels when I found you by the river. I'm trying to recruit more people to help our cause, but after the Delhi siege ended with so many cruel deaths as punishment by the British, I'm having a hard time convincing them."

"Why would you risk this?" I asked.

He just looked at me as the kids continued to sing nearby, covering our conversation.

I turned to Bhavani. "And you? You've found your sister finally."

"Chhaya didi is helping too. She introduced me to Tejinder Singh, the man you saw just now. And Javed, the fruit seller. And Charan, even though I had met him already on the boat. They're all trying to stop the East India Company by doing what little they can. They are the friends I was telling you about, Meera, risking everything for this cause. Chhaya didi is finding out what she can from the collector, but she doesn't have as many opportunities as we have."

"We?"

"Aren't you sick of playing house with the British? *I* don't want to play house with them. I want them out of our house."

I shook my head, brushing the stray hair out of my eyes and back into place behind my ears. "I'm not like you. I didn't have a loving father who taught me. I didn't go to school. I had no say in my life. I had no say in my future. Now I'm finally earning money to start a new life where I can have a say. I can't risk that all because you want revenge on the British."

"It isn't about revenge," Charan said. "It's about freedom. But I understand if it isn't your cause."

Bhavani shook her head. "It *should* be your cause. You want to save your own future. I want to save *our* future. For all Indians. You can stand guard outside the study as I try to find the papers we need. You can let me know when Memsahib or Cook or Captain Keene is coming."

I watched the group of happy kids who were now all dancing, carefree. I was finally in a position to have that kind of happiness again, without Krishna or Sheela or Babuji or sati to worry about. I couldn't risk that.

"I won't help," I said.

Bhavani's face fell.

"But I won't stand in your way."

Chapter 19

Bhavani burst through the back doors of the bungalow. I ran behind her, passing Salim, who was hanging laundry on the veranda, and set the empty birdcage down in its spot. The house was quiet without the occasional squawks from Lal, and I felt a lump in my throat, thinking about him . . . and how close I had been to getting caught by Krishna's brother and Sheela. But before I could dwell on either of those awful events, Bhavani looked around the empty hall, walked to the study, peered inside, and went right in.

I gasped, rushing after her, coming to an abrupt stop at the doorway so I didn't enter the study. I watched Bhavani inside, rifling through stacks of papers. "You better make sure they're in the same order you found them, or you'll get caught stealing," I whispered.

Bhavani moved a couple brown journals around. "I'm not stealing. *They're* the ones who've been stealing. Stealing food and fabric and money from everyone in this land. Oh, and they've stolen land too. Lots of it. And that emerald necklace Memsahib loves to wear? That's stolen too, most likely, when the British destroyed palaces and forts and took their jewels and diamonds. We have been looted."

I turned, eyeing Salim. He was too busy pulling the clothes off the line, his back to us, to notice me with my head in the study's doorway as Bhavani continued.

"Sepoy Charan wants to take the magazine. Just like in Delhi. Tejinder Singh is going to make sure he can get enough men to see that they are successful." Bhavani fanned through a handful of papers, scanning them. "They figured out which sepoys are on guard duty there, and when their shifts change, by spying on the magazine like when you saw them. But they need to know exactly where the cartridges are so they can get in and out fast," she said, moving a pile of Memsahib's journals to the side. "Captain Keene should have paperwork here with that information."

Just then the doors to the sitting room opened, and Memsahib emerged, looking backward as she called out. "Vinay! Have you seen my sketching pencil?"

"Bhavani!" I hissed, stepping back by the birdcage.

"One second . . ." she whispered, opening a folded-up page. "This might be it."

Vinay rushed to Memsahib from the sitting room, the fan tucked under his left arm, the pencil out-stretched in his right.

Memsahib took the pencil and turned to the veranda, spotting me. Her expression suddenly hardened as she noticed the empty birdcage.

"I'm sorry, Memsahib," I said, even shakier than when I had spoken to Salim. I was scared of what she was going to say to me about Lal. And I was terrified of what would happen to Bhavani if she didn't get out of the study fast. "I tried to catch Lal, but he got away." I took a few steps around Memsahib so my back was to the sitting room doors. She turned with me, no longer facing the study.

Memsahib let out a disappointed sigh. "Franny asked for a koel. It was all she wanted. Not a parrot. A koel. Dharamveer chased birds for days before he finally caught Lal, and now—" The sound of wood screeching on the floor came from the study.

She turned abruptly to the study behind her and pushed one of the doors open farther.

In the study, Bhavani was crouched on the ground, wiping the floor with a rag, a cover for what she'd actually been doing inside. "Sorry, Memsahib," she said. "I was wiping the floor and tripped on the desk leg."

Wrinkles formed on Memsahib's nose as she scowled. "Young lady, you seem to have a bad habit of going places you aren't allowed. First the magazine, and now this. Captain Keene's important work is in here. *My* important work is in here," she added so loudly it was as if she was trying to convince herself her work was as important as her husband's.

Bhavani rushed to the doorway. Memsahib moved to let her pass into the hall, and Bhavani exited the study, her head bowed down, acting far more subservient than she ever had before. "Please, Memsahib. I'm so sorry. Please don't flog me."

"I'm not the collector. The British are not all the same. It would be helpful if your lot remembered that."

Bhavani nodded, her shoulders drooping. "Please don't make me leave. I need this job." She looked up at me for a split second, and I could see there wasn't any

fear in her unflinching eyes, the way she was showing with the rest of her body. She was trying to make
Memsahib feel sorry for her so she wouldn't lose this
job. So she wouldn't lose access to the study.

Memsahib ran her fingers across the empty birdcage's bars. "You really should be let go. But you're
just an uneducated little girl. I know what your people
do to girls. You'll be married off, and then there's sati."

Bhavani's mouth opened like she wanted to correct Memsahib's assumption that every single person
in India believed in sati because the British had seen
that a few people did and then presumed Indians were
all the same.

From behind Memsahib, I shook my head vehe-
mently. Begging Bhavani to stop. To not talk back and
make things worse.

"All right," Memsahib said, speaking before
Bhavani could ruin her chances. "You may stay."

"Thank you, Memsahib," Bhavani did a namaste
and gratefully bowed her head again.

"But outside," Memsahib added.

"What?" Bhavani looked up.

"I can't trust you in the house, dear. You can wash
the dishes on the veranda, take care of the laundry,

and work in the garden from now on." Memsahib glanced outside. "Winter's around the corner. You may want to do yourself a favor and use some of your hard-earned wages on a good shawl. Oh, and happy Diwali, girls."

With that, Memsahib headed out to the garden to draw, and Salim quickly moved out of her way.

Chapter 20

After I had finished cleaning up the Keenes' dinner that night, I brought the dishes out to the veranda to Bhavani. In the distance, several homes that celebrated the holiday were lit up with Diwali lamps, and in the distance, we could hear celebratory singing. I crouched next to her, helping her pour the container of well water onto the dirty plates and spoons while she scrubbed them.

"You're going to have to do it now, you know," Bhavani said, handing me a washed teacup.

I shook my head. "I don't want to get caught." I pointed to the indigo pouch at my waist. "This is a quarter full. I need this job to start my new life." I scrubbed at a little bowl, wiping a stray okra seed off the outside. "And more than that, I need to stay safe."

Bhavani put a plate down on the veranda loudly. It rattled briefly and then settled.

I sighed. "I didn't tell you this, but I saw my husband's brother and his wife today. Right before Lal flew off at the jeweler's."

Bhavani wound the bottom of one of her braids around her finger.

"This is her hometown," I continued, putting my dish down much more gently than Bhavani. "I had convinced myself I was safe here at Captain Keene's house. That my future—that I want a say in—was safe. That my father and Krishna's family could never find me. But that's not true. I won't be safe until this pouch is full. Until I have enough money to leave this town and go far away from my past. I can't risk that for your cause."

"It's your cause too. I told you that." Bhavani pushed the stack of clay vessels forward to wash them, and I took half. "Your pouch full of money isn't going to buy you real freedom. But I guess on some level, I get why Charan said he understands if it isn't your cause. I didn't really care about rebelling earlier. I barely bothered looking at the East India Company men in my town before my father died." Bhavani poured water on the dishes.

"My father worked hard every day to earn enough money to send Chhaya didi and me to school. But the British East India Company policies in our town were hurting everyone. Our neighbors and relatives worked hard constructing roads and buildings for them, weaving intricate designs into rich fabrics for them, growing food for them, like beasts of burden. And they were being taxed so much, they didn't have enough left to eat. Chhaya didi and I ate every day, so we never thought our immediate family was in danger. Then when some East India Company officers and their families came to town, Didi saw one of them had a little girl, who must have been Victoria. My father told her to take the opportunity to go live with them as their ayah."

Bhavani put the dishes out to dry on a big piece of cotton fabric and stood up. I followed her through the garden as she continued.

"A few months after Chhaya didi left, I saw my father shivering. When he took his kurta off, I saw that his ribs were protruding through his body, like the stripes on a tiger, just like those laborers who build roads. He'd been giving me and Chhaya didi all the food, starving himself to ensure we were fed for weeks. I had no idea." Bhavani kicked a rock out of the way. "It was awful. Do you know what it's like to go hungry?"

I shook my head. Other than the day I had run away, I hadn't ever felt true hunger.

"Your mouth feels dry all the time. Your head hurts nonstop. He had been hiding all those symptoms from me for months. Hiding the fact that he was so weak he couldn't lift his arms over his head because they felt as heavy as rocks. Hiding how cold he was anytime the slightest breeze went by, because he had no fat on his bones to keep him warm."

Bhavani's voice cracked, and a lump formed in my throat. I felt terrible for her and what she saw her father go through.

"When I tried to get him to eat a few grains of food, he couldn't, because his body was trying to inhale it instead of swallowing it, and he would choke. All just to keep my sister and me alive."

Bhavani ran her hand down the bark of the tree outside our little home. A few houses down, Prasad and his friends were laughing and eating a Diwali meal out on their cots. "All because of the British East India Company."

I followed Bhavani into our house, thinking about how my own father thought so little of me he was ready to escort me to my death for the sake of honor. Would he have given me all his food during a famine so I could live?

Bhavani stood in the corner of our home. "And then . . . he died."

"I'm so sorry," I said softly.

She shook her head. "They are the ones who should be sorry. They're still doing it to Indians all across the land. I don't want another child to lose their father to starvation because of them. I don't want anyone else to think things are fine because they see some healthy people but don't see what's happening to the ones who are hurting. I want the East India Company out before they hurt one more person."

I looked at Bhavani, at the fire in her eyes. Suddenly, I wanted to be like her. I wanted to be brave. I wanted her to think I was as fierce as her. I just didn't know if I was, though.

"I'll do it," I said before I could stop the words from spilling out.

Bhavani beamed. She nodded at me, tears filling her eyes as she reached out and squeezed my shoulder.

Then someone shouted outside: "Bhavani didi!"

Vinay came in with a lantern—leading Chhaya, whose head and shoulders were wrapped in a shawl. Its shadow covered much of her face, but I could see she was shaking. She fell to her knees, and the shawl slipped off her head. Her lip was bleeding.

We rushed to her side. "What happened?" Bhavani asked.

Chhaya trembled, eyeing Vinay like she wasn't sure how much she could say in front of him. "The collector found me going through his files. I told him I was looking for paper for Victoria to draw on. He told me next time I better ask, not go through his belongings . . . and then to make sure I remembered, he—he flogged me." She collapsed into her lap, burying her face in her hands.

I took the lantern from Vinay in the doorway and held it up to Chhaya. As she sobbed into her palms, the pallu of her white sari on her head fell to the side, revealing her back, just above her blouse. A dark red gash crossed her back diagonally above the thin cotton blouse, and through it, as Chhaya's blood seeped into the blouse, a stain that couldn't wash out.

December 1857

Chapter 21

*O*ver the next few weeks, Bhavani spent the early morning hours applying turmeric to Chhaya's wounds over at the collector's property, or checking in on her before rushing back to start our job at the Keene residence. She couldn't risk getting into any more trouble and totally lose her access to the property.

And I couldn't find the courage to enter the study and find what the rebels needed.

Bhavani and I headed up the veranda, the first whispers of winter all around us. She reached for my arm, stopping me before I got within earshot of Abbu, who was crouched over the dishes, washing them at the corner of the veranda.

"Javed bhaiya and Tejinder bhaiya came by early this morning, when I was leaving Chhaya didi at the collector's," Bhavani said, calling both men the respectful term for a big brother.

I shuddered at the thought of the collector. "Why is she continuing to work for that awful man?"

"Because she knows how important the cause is."

I swallowed hard as Bhavani continued. "Javed told us there's been a lot of movement at the barracks. The sepoys are heading out, including Charan, and Captain Keene is going to go too. If the opportunity comes up, you have to take it."

I turned to Bhavani as thunder rumbled above us, warning us of what was to come, despite it being a month and a half since the monsoon season had ended. I rubbed my back at the spot where Chhaya had been flogged. My shoulders felt heavy, like I was being forced to carry a burden Bhavani had passed on to me. A burden I had not chosen for myself.

I searched for the words to tell Bhavani I wasn't as fearless as her. That I wasn't sure if I had agreed to help her because I wanted her to think of me as her equal or because I truly believed in risking my life for this cause. That I felt scared about going into the study when I could lose my job or my life. That I wasn't sure I could do this . . .

When a rare December rain suddenly began to pour.

In front of us, Memsahib ran up the stone stairs, clutching her journal as she ran inside to the study. She hadn't spoken to me much since the Diwali day we lost Lal. But she was talking to Bhavani even less, not even bothering to make eye contact with her.

I gave Bhavani an apologetic look, as she was not allowed to enter the house, and rushed inside to dry off as Dharamveer began closing the shutters on the barred windows.

The captain walked by me in the hall, followed by Vinay. He paused at the squeaking study door. "I'll be gone for a few days with the sepoys. You make sure Memsahib is taken care of."

I nodded as the two of them went into the study. Memsahib greeted the captain with a frown. It was the same scowl Ma would give Babuji when he talked about a woman's role in the world and how little use women and girls had other than cooking and raising children. Vinay shut the study doors, but I could still hear Memsahib and the captain arguing loudly in English. I recognized a couple of the words from when Bhavani had translated English during breakfast with the nawab for me: *"Rebel scum."*

I walked into the kitchen, where Abbu had gone after washing the dishes. A few minutes later, I was pouring new oil into the lamp when I heard doors slam on the other side of the house. Captain Keene must have left for Delhi.

Abbu handed me a cup of tea, bread and jam, and an omelet on a plate. I took the tray up to the study. The green doors were once again open, and Memsahib stood before a stack of brown journals on the edge of the desk, counting them. One journal lay open next to the pile.

"That can't be right," Memsahib said, counting the pile again as the sounds of rain pattered in the garden outside the lone window behind her. She plopped back down at her desk and motioned for me to enter the room.

I set the food down next to Memsahib, being careful to avoid the papers strewn on the other side of the desk. I glanced at them, but they were full of words I couldn't read, and there was no way I could grab them in front of Memsahib. Besides, Bhavani would have taken all the paper if that was what the rebels needed. But they didn't. They only wanted papers on the magazine.

Memsahib reached for the chai. Her face was blotchy, and I could see the tracks where tears had traveled down her red cheeks. "Thank you," she said softly, moving her pencil aimlessly across the journal drawing of an unfinished petal. "I can't believe he left today of all days."

I glanced at the paper pile near the now-empty tray. My hand was shaking, but I slowly reached for the tray, thinking I could grab the sheet right underneath it. I grazed the paper with my index finger and tucked it under the tray while the rest of my fingers gripped the tray's handle.

"It's a bougainvillea," Memsahib said.

I stopped, releasing the paper. "Ji, Memsahib?" I squeaked.

"The leaf you're staring at. I was trying to draw a bougainvillea—but the rain. I had to stop. The magenta ones were Franny's favorite. And today is her birthday. *Was* her birthday. So . . ." she trailed off.

My chest felt heavy for Memsahib. I knew that look in her eyes. It was the same look in Ma's eyes—the look she'd tried to cover up after Ravi died. But the sadness was still there, a tiny salty tear that wanted to escape. I hated that look.

So I abandoned the paper and the tray and ran out through the kitchen, out the back doors, grabbing my sandals and passing Bhavani—who was huddled where the roof gave a little shelter to the veranda, trying to get some relief from the rain.

"Did you get it?" she softly called out.

I shook my head.

"Don't run scared," she whispered, rushing to my side. "You'll make them suspicious."

"I'm not," I whispered back, coming to a stop at the sprawling magenta bougainvillea tree. But the thorny branches were still too high for me, and the petals all over the ground were old and crushed. I climbed onto the wet trunk of the tree next door to the bougainvillea, pushing myself up with my right foot, but I slipped and slid to the ground.

I brushed the browned leaves from the ground off my sari and tried again. This time I made sure to hold the branch tighter and not depend only on my feet. I took a deep breath, then got a few feet up the tree, reached for the pokey bougainvillea branch, and snapped it off. I held the branch with two fingers, avoiding the thorns, and scooted back down, shivering, right as the chilly rain stopped as suddenly as it had started.

Safely on the ground, I ran past Bhavani and back up the veranda. I wiped my muddy sandals off on the veranda stones, kicked them to the side, and made my way to the study.

Memsahib was finishing up her breakfast as I placed the small bougainvillea branch before her, accidentally sprinkling a couple raindrops on the table. She gasped and ran her finger across the dewy flowers. "For me?"

I nodded, my teeth chattering. The rainwater in my sari blouse grew cold against my skin. "For Franny's birthday."

For an instant, Memsahib's eyes welled up, and I was afraid she would cry. But she sniffled once and composed herself, clearing her throat as she fiddled with her string of pearls, making the emerald glisten. "You're drenched. You must be freezing." She pushed her chair out and stood up. "Come with me."

I followed her into the sitting room. Salim crouched on the floor, cleaning it while being careful to avoid breaking the strange statues of horses and men's heads that were scattered around the room. Vinay was dusting the corner table.

"Vinay, get her a towel," Memsahib called out. "Quickly."

Vinay rushed out the side door and returned with a towel. I wrapped it around my body and wiped my head, slowly feeling warm again.

Memsahib bent down and opened a cupboard. She dug past several wooden rattles and stacks of clothes, emerging with a white kite with the blue silhouette of a flying bird painted on it.

She started to hand it to me but stopped, running her fingers over the thin paper like she was petting a real bird. She cleared her throat, blinking fast, and turned the kite to show me the bird on it. "I got this kite at the Taj Mahal, almost ten years ago. It was when the captain and I first arrived in India. It was when I first met the collector, actually. I watched in horror as he and his wife and a dozen other civil servants danced in the Taj Mahal. Dancing in front of the tomb of a dead queen. Can you imagine?"

I shook my head. I had never seen the Taj Mahal, but Radha Chachi had told me many stories about how an emperor had built it to honor his dead wife. I guessed he'd thought a lot higher of her than Babuji thought of Ma or me.

Memsahib traced the bird on the kite with her finger. "I was so appalled I left the party and headed outside to go sketch some flowers. A young boy was there, selling kites. He told me his ancestors had made kites for the emperors of Agra." She smiled knowingly. "I'm sure he made that story up. But I bought the kite from him anyway. I overpaid too, helping him. Helping that child. And thought that one day I'd fly this kite with my own child."

She cleared her throat. "This was going to be Franny's birthday present. Before . . . before she left us. But it seems unnatural, having it cooped up in here forever. So I want you to have it."

I shook my head. "I can't—"

But Memsahib put the kite in my hand. "It should be with someone who can use it." She turned so I couldn't see her face. "Now go on. Back to work," she added, her voice quivering as she headed into the bedroom and closed the doors.

I walked back to the study. I rushed to the desk, the kite in my hand. This was my chance. With Memsahib in her room, I could grab the paper with the tray. I could maybe grab more than one.

I lifted up the tray, revealing the papers underneath. I touched the top page again and suddenly remembered the bloody gash in Chhaya's shoulder. My hands felt cold and clammy, and I abandoned the paper, stepped back into the hall with the tray and kite, and pulled the two study doors shut.

Memsahib would be back here soon to finish sketching the bougainvillea. And she had given me this kite. I couldn't risk hurting her on Franny's birthday. Ma wouldn't want me to do that to another mother who had lost a child. I turned, catching Bhavani's eyes on the veranda, as Dharamveer opened the shutters. She stared at the kite in my hand, at the bird's silhouette.

I ran my finger over the frame of the kite. It was almost like I had gotten Ravi's kite back. Like I had gotten my family back. I gave Bhavani a small smile. And although she didn't return it, I didn't care. My heart felt lighter than it had in days. It felt as light as a feather.

January 1858

Chapter 22

"*You know Memsahib doesn't* think of you as a daughter, right?" Bhavani asked, holding a lantern to show us the tree line behind the servant quarters, as the burning orange sun started to dip.

The crisp January air was circling around me, chilly, like Bhavani's eyes when she asked the question, which she had every day for weeks now. I paused, clenching my toes into the dry dirt below, as I kept my arms protectively over the kite Memsahib had given me. I had flown it by myself while Bhavani checked in on Chhaya or met with Sepoy Charan, Tejinder, Javed, and a handful of other men from town who had joined the resistance. But this time, Bhavani was with me. Because this time we weren't playing.

"She doesn't really," Bhavani added, turning back, shining the lantern at me until I caught up to her. "If she thought of you as family, as her equal—if any of them did—they would come here as equals, as guests, as friends, not as rulers who scammed us out of money, food, and jewels."

Bhavani ran through the trees, braids flying, still talking about the East India Company. I quickened my pace to follow. "They wouldn't think their way of doing things was better than ours. They wouldn't look down on our clothes, our religions, our languages, our culture. They wouldn't think they had a right to take our riches and bleed our land dry and starve us and tax us and trade our goods, all to make their lives better even if it makes ours so much worse."

"I know that." I struggled to catch up while also trying hard not to get poked by the branches or trip over the vines. "I was going to play pachisi with Abbu tonight, but instead I'm here, helping you, aren't I?" I huffed, almost slipping in a mossy patch.

"Keep up," Bhavani said. "We only have a few minutes before it gets dark and we look strange with a kite. You haven't been able to get into the study—"

"Not alone," I interrupted, sensing she didn't quite

believe my excuses. But they were true. Memsahib was either inside the study, or the doors were closed, or she was heading back to the study. And I had already tried to find the papers, hadn't I? But what use was it when I couldn't read?

"I'm doing double the work inside with you gone, you know," I added, hoping it would convince Bhavani that I was trying to be like her, even if I didn't truly feel like her, or even think like her about the cause. How could I, when putting myself at risk was the exact opposite of staying safe, earning money, and getting to start a new life? The indigo pouch bounced against my waist, reminding me of my own goals.

"We're almost up the hill. Remember, if anyone catches us, we pretend we got lost trying to fly this kite."

I nodded, trying to straighten my spine and stand tall. I tried to seem like I could be brave on my own, even if I hadn't managed to find the papers in the study and was only daring when Bhavani was by my side.

But even with Bhavani here, I felt nervous. I was not in the mood to find out if this hill was truly haunted like everyone talked about.

With the sunlight now faded enough that we actually needed the lantern, Bhavani pushed through some overgrown grass on the other side of the trees. As the forest cleared, she held her lantern up to luminate the old bungalow at the top of the hill. Its gray paint was peeling, and hundreds of vines grew up its sides like hands from the netherworld, reaching, grabbing, refusing to let go. Thick, sticky cobwebs ran across the porch columns, shielding the house like mysterious veils, their centers filled with the hollowed-out shells of deceased insects. As we entered the bungalow's front yard, I could see dust and dirt all over the porch, like it hadn't been cleaned in ages. But there were fresh footprints in the dust, leading to and from the door.

I shivered. "Whose house is it?"

"Nobody's. It's empty. Look at it." She ran up the porch and wiped at one of the windows, peering in.

I stayed a safe distance back. "Why didn't the captain tear it down and build something new here?" I whispered. From the hill I could see clusters of homes on one side and the river on the other, reflecting the last shimmers of the dying sun. It seemed to me to be a better location than the bungalow's placement down the hill. But maybe it truly was haunted. I wouldn't want to live in a haunted house.

"Looks like he's using it for storage," Bhavani

whispered back. "There's just a bunch of old furniture in here." She inhaled deeply. "Smells like sandalwood. I thought there might have been something here that would be helpful to the rebellion."

The house stood eerily on the hill like a spooky watchman. Another shiver ran down my spine. "Bhavani, let's get out of here. The ghost on the hill lives here!"

Snickering, Bhavani ran toward me. "Come on, Meera. You're such a silly girl. That story is just to keep people away from this hill. Do you see any ghosts?"

I shook my head, my heart still thumping loudly in my throat.

She looked at the sun dipping on the horizon. "We had another setback. But we have to keep at it. I'm not much use when there isn't much that is useful out here," she added. "But you're inside. And Captain Keene is still gone. You have to find out where the cartridges are so the rebels can take them."

Before I could answer, a gust of wind tugged at the kite. The fluttering sound of the paper rattled against its frame in the wind. *Dhadak-dhadak-dhadak*, like a heartbeat.

Like my brother's heartbeat.

I held the kite protectively. Bhavani was relying too much on me being lucky, like I would become the one villager who would truly have something to celebrate on the nawab's birthday. "There was this story of the nawab of our town," I started, "who sewed coins into his kite and flew it out into the village each year on his birthday."

Bhavani laughed. "Don't tell me you believed that story, Meera. Every kingdom says its king or nawab did that. It's just a myth. How would a kite fly with heavy coins in it? And how would you sew a pocket to a paper kite?"

My ears burned. I felt foolish. Was everything Babuji said about me not being worthy of an education true?

Before I could defend myself, a loud squeak caught my ear. I turned toward the abandoned bungalow behind us, where the front doors had swung open. There, the shadow of a towering man holding a hurricane lantern could be seen right before the sun disappeared.

It was Captain Keene. He must have come back from Delhi. He thundered in English, leering over us, his hands gesturing wildly.

I could tell he wanted to know why we were there. I opened my mouth to tell him we were just flying a kite, but no words came out. Even Bhavani seemed a little scared.

"What is wrong with you people? I show you a little kindness, and you think you can run all over my property? My land?" he said even louder, in Hindi.

"I'm so sorry," I mumbled, tears trickling down my cheeks.

"Get out of this yard, foolish girls. Didn't Vinay tell you? You're not allowed on this hill. Is that clear?"

Bhavani and I nodded.

"And don't forget your place," Captain Keene spat.

Spring 1858

Chapter 23

I spent the rest of winter with my head down, staring at my feet. I scrubbed the floors, the dishes, the walls; prepared food, served food, served the Keenes; and never dared to set foot in the study unless Memsahib called me there. She had convinced the captain that Bhavani must have been the reason we were on the hill. She made some joke about Bhavani having an "explorer's bug" and thinking she was part of the East India Company.

I did as I was told and remembered my place, just like I had with Babuji, staying out of his class. Just like I had with the wedding that had been arranged before I could talk, let alone agree or disagree. Just like I always had, except for the one time

I hadn't, the one time I'd run, the one time Bhavani said didn't really matter.

As spring arrived, the pouch I wore at my waist grew three-quarters full of coins. Based on what Bhavani had taught me, that meant by summer, I would be able to leave the Keenes and go find a place far from here to live. Bhavani would be upset I hadn't gotten what the rebels needed, and I wasn't sure I'd manage on my own without her, but maybe I could hold my head up high knowing I had tried to help her. Maybe I could find something I was good at doing and earn a living. Maybe I would get to stop taking orders from everyone around me the way I had my whole life. I would miss seeing Memsahib every morning as I served her breakfast. I would miss getting to see what she was drawing in her journals, or hearing how excited she was to send them to a publisher in England soon.

I wouldn't miss all the questions she had asked about sati, though.

Now I stood under the shade of the blooming gulmohar tree in the garden next to Memsahib, who was seated in a chair, sketching away furiously in her journal. Bhavani was hanging wet laundry on one of the many laundry lines on the veranda, having finally given up trying to figure out why Captain Keene had been in the old bungalow the day he caught us, instead deciding he must have been dumping some more old furniture there.

"Is this what it's like, do you think?" Memsahib asked, showing me a horrific sketch of a woman sitting on a burning pyre, her mouth stretched out in agony as she screamed silently.

My stomach dropped, and my hands started to sweat. "I'm not . . . sure," I said slowly.

Memsahib frowned. "Is the mouth wrong?"

I shook my head as a fly buzzed around my nose, not wanting to remember the terrible thing I had escaped. "I don't know."

"Silly girl. Didn't you pay attention to your world before you came here? Every family here does this. Surely you've seen several of these vulgar events."

I wanted to tell Memsahib every family didn't do this. That I came from one of the few families that did take part in such an awful tradition. But I didn't correct her. I just said sorry and swatted at the fly, my hand accidentally knocking into a branch and sending a shower of reddish-orange petals and pollen down onto my head.

"If I can get this image right," Memsahib continued, shading in the fire under the burning woman, "this book will be so popular back in England. You know, my mother was *aghast* when my father told her we were moving here when I was about your age. Because of sati. She went on and on about how backward everything was here." She let out a little chuckle. "Everyone acts horrified, but the truth is, they love to read this kind of stuff about primitive cultures."

I nodded, remembering a lesson Babuji had given his class of boys that I could barely hear, about all the inventions and advancements in math and science that had come from this land.

Then I shook my head, trying to get pollen and petals out without smearing them, thinking about how strange it was for Memsahib to be telling the story of people in this land when she didn't actually know it. Shouldn't we tell our own story?

"That's going to be in your hair forever." Memsahib laughed, finally looking at me instead of her drawing. "Bend down here."

I hesitantly crouched by Memsahib in her chair, my feet feeling like they weighed more than an elephant. Memsahib began to gently brush the dust off my scalp.

"Franny had the softest golden ringlets, but they would get so knotted during the monsoon. I used to just give up on untangling them and put a flower in her hair to pretend she looked civilized." Memsahib paused. "And she'd always insist I wear one too. She said it made me look like a lady," she added softly.

I nodded, feeling Memsahib's fingers all over my head, like Ma's long ago. The year I was seven, she had found me crying after Babuji yelled at me for breaking a clay pot balanced on my head. I had been doing a poor job of imitating the women who effortlessly balanced heavy water vessels on their heads at the well. Ma had gently explained how we couldn't afford to break dishes and asked me to try balancing marigolds on my head instead. That night and for months after, she'd had to pull a lot of petals out of my hair, but she didn't mind.

My chest grew tight, missing all the tiny moments with Ma. Going to the bazaar, grinding lentils and grains, slicing vegetables, gathering water. It wasn't raining, but I felt like I was drowning in a shower of memories.

"You're all set," Memsahib said, brushing her hands together.

I blinked quickly, afraid I would start to cry.

"Oh, one more thing," Memsahib said, breaking two small yellow flowers off a little plant next to us.

She tucked a flower behind my ear. It wavered for a second, top-heavy from the large petals, but then settled. Then she put the other yellow flower in her hair and smiled, glancing up at the sky like she was staring at a loved one before turning back to me. "Perfect. Now you look like a lady."

Memsahib walked back up the veranda, past Bhavani, and headed into the house.

The petals caressed my cheekbone. The flower felt soft. Like a gentle touch. Almost like a mother's touch. I started to smile but caught Bhavani's eye.

"Just because she's doing your hair like her daughter," Bhavani said, yanking the captain's shirt off the line, "doesn't mean you're her—"

"I know that!" I shouted, surprised at how loudly I was defending myself. I obviously knew I wasn't Memsahib's daughter. I was Ma's daughter. Smart, caring, strong Ma, who just wasn't strong enough to protect me. I walked up to the veranda. "You're just upset because you've been working outside for all these months."

"No. I'm upset because you're such a weakling. You couldn't do the one job you were asked to do because you so enjoy being Memsahib's pet."

I yanked Memsahib's poofy dress off the line and threw it into the basket next to Bhavani, grabbing the flower as it fell out of my hair. "I'm not her pet. I just . . . I know what it's like to see a child die. My baby brother died."

Some of the harshness blinked out of her eyes. "I'm sorry. I didn't know—"

"You never asked. You never asked anything about me other than sati and my sister-in-law. You don't know how strict my father is. Or how my mother didn't even fight to save me from sati."

Bhavani frowned. "You never told me anything, either. I told you all about my father and Chhaya didi."

I felt the soft flower petals in my hand. "I've been trying to find the information," I said, not sure if I was being fully truthful. "You didn't find the papers, and you had been searching too. It's not easy. And I'm not weak. I ran away when I was asked to commit sati."

"Yes, I've heard that several times before," Bhavani

said, shaking the wrinkles out of a wet pair of Captain Keene's pants. "And that was great, Meera. Really. It was brave and strong and showed what you're capable of. But other people are suffering under the British just like you were under your family's strict beliefs. Our movement is falling apart. Charan has been out with the other sepoys, marching around who knows what parts of India. And Javed bhaiya has gone missing. Tejinder bhaiya says he thinks the East India Company arrested him."

My throat tightened. I hadn't met Javed many times, but I didn't want him to be hurt. "That just goes to show you how dangerous this is. Men aren't safe. So what makes you think you are? Do you want to end up flogged like Chhaya or worse? We are free here. We are safe, even if it is temporary. I almost died in September. I won't take my safety for granted. Don't you get how important that is?"

Bhavani scoffed. "I knew it. So you're not really trying to get in the study, are you?"

"I want my freedom. I can't risk that . . ." I trailed off.

"Don't you get the difference between your freedom from sati and your father, and true freedom? Not being ordered around by *anyone* who thinks they own your life?"

"Of course I do. I'm not going to be at this bungalow forever. This is just temporary."

Bhavani shook her head. "This isn't temporary. As long as they're here as colonizers, this isn't temporary, Meera. Their decisions will decide if we live or die."

"Not for me," I replied. "As soon as this pouch is full, I'll be making my own decisions."

A koel chirped above us. I turned away from Bhavani, hoping it was Lal.

"How?" Bhavani scoffed. "All you do is follow. You follow your parents, me, Memsahib, a bird—"

"That's not true. I can think for myself." I squinted, trying to catch sight of the koel's feet in the mango trees above. My shoulders slumped. There was no bell on his foot.

"You're so busy worrying about birds instead of important things," Bhavani sputtered. "Know what your precious koels do?"

I took a step back.

"When they're ready to lay an egg, they sneak into a crow's nest and lay it there, so that the mother crow does all the work sitting on the egg, and then all the work feeding the bird when it hatches. Does that sound honest and cute to you? Or maybe it sounds exactly like what Memsahib and everyone else in the East India Company are doing. Entering someone else's nest and stealing from the birds who live there."

"Leave Lal out of this."

"Why? Having a hard time accepting someone you adore could be so bad?"

"No," I said, giving the wicker basket a little kick. "He's not bad. I know for a fact Lal would never do that."

"Oh, you do? Did Lal tell you? Do you speak bird now? Did you learn that in school?"

I blinked back tears. Bhavani knew I wanted desperately to go to school. Her words were mean and unfair. "No. I know for a fact because Lal is male."

"So?"

"Males don't lay eggs," I said triumphantly, head held high as I entered the bungalow Bhavani couldn't set foot in and shut the back doors.

I rushed into the kitchen, tucking the flower back in its place behind my ear as I sat down to help Abbu make dough for the double roti the captain enjoyed.

"Everything okay?" he asked.

I poured a little oil into the dough, pretending everything was okay, pretending my heartbeat wasn't thumping in my throat. I obviously knew Memsahib wasn't my mother. I might not have gone to school, but I wasn't foolish. But what was the harm in pretending for a split second if it made me happy?

I frowned, and the slight movement made the yellow flower behind my ear fall to the ground. I picked it up and slid it back behind my ear, but no matter how I tried to steady it, as soon as I moved, the flower would flop back to the kitchen floor. Its petals had turned translucent and limp, bits of grime from the floor now staining the yellow.

I could pretend all I wanted, but the flower was not going to cooperate. I stood up and tossed it out the window, then went back to the dough, leaving the once-vibrant flower to wilt in its own earth.

April 1858

Chapter 24

*W*hile a pair of parrots chirped in a plumeria tree in the garden, like they couldn't stop singing about the fresh April morning air, I scrubbed hard at one of the clay dishes piling up on the veranda next to Abbu. Our breakfast duties were done, but there was a lot of cooking ahead of us since the captain was having several officers and officials over tonight for a Friday dinner of Indian food.

"Careful. You'll break them," he said, gently taking the clay vessel from my hand to dry on the cotton cloth next to him.

Down in the garden, Bhavani walked by the kitchen window with some freshly cut flowers to give Cook for the dining room vases. "She doesn't mind if things get hurt, Abbu. As long as *she's* okay." She plopped the flowers into Cook's hand, which was waving, all red and sweaty, out the window.

I glared at Bhavani. We hadn't been talking much since our fight a couple weeks ago. Poor Vinay was stuck sleeping between us in our little home, and on some days, when Bhavani seemed extra annoyed with me, she'd tell Vinay to relay messages like, "Tell Meera to stop breathing so loudly. I can't sleep with all the noise she makes."

"Still fighting?" Abbu shook his head. "Isn't there enough fighting in this land? You know Rani Lakshmibai's Jhansi was attacked by the British. A huge battle is going on right now over there."

My stomach turned. Was she going to be okay? How would she fight back against so many men?

"So much bloodshed." Abbu coughed into his shoulder. There were more specks of blood on his white kurta.

"Abbu . . ." I said, pointing to his shoulder, worried.

But he just smiled. "I told you, it happens. Nothing to worry about. My Fatima wrote me, telling me to come home, but—"

A loud, guttural scream startled us.

I scanned the garden for the source before turning back to Abbu.

He shook his head. "It's something down on the street. I heard they had caught a rebel. It's best not to go—"

But Bhavani was already running past the veranda through the garden.

I had to go too. I had to make sure it wasn't Tejinder, Javed, or Charan. I wiped my wet hands on my waist and rushed down the veranda steps and through the garden. Bhavani was just ahead, and I followed her to the brick wall, where the two guards stood at the side gate. I pushed my way past Prasad and the other curious servants until I was at the front of the iron gate door, next to Bhavani.

Sepoys were marching through the street toward us. "Let us out so we can see," Bhavani told the guards.

One of them shook his head, the gray hairs in his mustache shaking along with him. "It's not safe."

I glanced around quickly for Vinay. From the way my insides were wobbling, something bad was going to happen, and he shouldn't see it.

But he wasn't out here.

"This is what happens when you think of

rebelling!" Captain Keene shouted from a brown horse at the front of the regiment, as hundreds of bystanders gawked on the side of the road. "When you think of stealing or destroying what is the rightful property of the East India Company! When you think of acting like Rani Lakshmibai, who dares to defy us!"

I had never seen the captain marching through town like this.

Behind Captain Keene, two sepoys had a tight grip on the elbows of a man with a curly black mustache. His arms were bound behind his back with chains, and the sepoys pulled him forward, his feet dragging behind. His face was swollen and puffy with splotches of blue and green bruises around his gray eyes. And his hairline was crusted with dry blood.

"It's Javed bhaiya," Bhavani whispered to me, crumpled, diagonal creases of worry across her forehead.

My throat tightened. Javed had been caught. They would hang him for sure.

Javed screamed the same hoarse scream we'd heard moments earlier. "We will not be silenced!"

A hand covered my eyes, and all I could hear was Javed's moan as someone must have hit him. I pulled the fingers off and turned to see Abbu standing behind me, trying to protect me from the awful sight.

"You girls should not be here," he said, his voice quivering.

Captain Keene paused dramatically in the road for all the townspeople who had gathered to see. "See what happens when you have foolish thoughts of rebellion?" he shouted so loudly his voice cracked. "Look at what's happening to your dear rani of Jhansi right now, running for her life! Look what will happen to this rebel!"

A sepoy next to Javed hit him across the face. Javed spat out a tooth as blood dribbled down his mouth. He shook his head like he was trying to recover from the impact and looked up again just as he was dragged past the iron gate.

Bhavani reached through the iron gate, but I grabbed her wrist and pulled it back, shaking my head at her.

"He saw me," Bhavani whispered. "I just—I just wanted to let him know I cared. That I didn't want this to happen to him."

"He knows that," I said, my voice catching in my throat.

"Tejinder Singh has gone!" Javed shouted, as if to no one in particular. But I knew he was trying to give Bhavani a message. His voice grew fainter, carried away by the wind. "He's gone to spread the flames of rebellion from town to town. We will not be silenced. We will not be si—"

Another white man with long, wispy brown sideburns hit Javed hard across the face. Javed's head slumped, bobbing along as he was dragged out of our sight like the last bounces of a skipping stone before it sank into the river for good.

Near the end of the dozens and dozens of rows of sepoys marching behind Javed, I noticed one was looking sideways instead of straight ahead, right at the side gate to the Keenes' property where we stood. It was Charan.

Bhavani opened her mouth to say something, but he just shook his head helplessly, the fire in his eyes doused, as he begged her to remain silent.

She turned to me, tears running down her face. "We have to do something," she said softly.

I knew this was wrong. It had to be stopped. But there was no way we could do it. There was no way I could risk getting caught trying to find information for the rebels. What was happening to Javed was even worse than what happened to Chhaya. Captain Keene was giving us all a warning, and I couldn't ignore it.

"There's nothing we can do," I whispered back to Bhavani. "Even Charan can't stop this. He's out-numbered. *We* are outnumbered."

Bhavani kicked the iron gate and grabbed my wrist. "Come with me." She pulled me through the mass of servants. Some of them were dispersing and heading back to their jobs. "We don't have a lot of time."

Chapter 25

Inside our quarters, Bhavani made sure no one outside was close enough to overhear, then sat on the floor and pulled a brown journal out from under one of the mattresses. "Look at this," she said. "Take it. Open it." She waved the book at me.

But my hand wouldn't leave my side to take it. I sank to my knees, my voice dropping to a whisper. "That's one of Memsahib's journals."

Bhavani nodded. "I got it the last time I was in the study. Before she kicked me out."

This was why Memsahib was counting her journals over and over again on Franny's birthday. "She knows it's missing," I said, barely able to get the words out, as a nervous fluttering crept through my insides.

"I couldn't find Captain Keene's papers on the magazine that day. But I thought maybe something she had written could be helpful to the movement. I had given it to Charan, but he sent it back to Chhaya this morning, passed through the few rebels left." Bhavani sighed, picking at a loose white thread where her sari sat on her knee. "He must have known they had caught Javed and it wasn't safe to have this anymore. I don't think anything in there helped either. I went all the way through it this morning, hoping there was something of use, but there isn't," she added, adjusting her pallu on her head.

I stood back up, shaking my head at what was happening to Javed right now for trying to stop the British East India Company. "I'm not touching that. Give it back to her," I said, my pulse thumping in my throat.

Bhavani stood up and raised her chin. *"You* can give it back. After you take a good look at it." She practically spat those last words out as she tossed the journal to my side of the mattress, where it rested in a beam of sunshine from the doorway. "It may not help the rebellion, but maybe, just maybe, it can help you," she muttered, storming out.

I heard Prasad's voice as a group of men passed by outside on their way to the garden, so I grabbed the journal and ducked into the corner, where Franny's kite was propped up. It was still bright enough here to see the journal, but hopefully no one would notice me holding it.

As I waited for my heart to stop pounding so loud I was certain Memsahib could hear it back in the bungalow, I ran my fingers over the rough edges of the paper inside. What had she written?

I couldn't read. Bhavani could, and she knew I couldn't. So she must have been talking about the drawings.

I opened the book and glanced at the first page. There was a drawing of a young British child around two, with ringlets and a dress. It must have been Franny. There were words below the image, but of course I couldn't read them.

I flipped through more pages. There were drawings of the magazine and the sepoys in front of it. This must have been why Bhavani had thought it could be useful. On the next page were sketches of the barracks and sepoys. Then there were a few pages of kingfishers, crows, parrots, an owl, a snake, and a donkey. There was page after page after page of drawings of flowers and plants.

I continued to leaf through the diary. There were drawings of ayahs holding babies, a village full of naked children running, almost like the collector had described, and sketch after sketch of the various stalls and tents at the market. There was a page full of beautiful drawings of a Jain temple, a Sikh gurudwara, a Muslim mosque, and a Hindu temple. On the next page, Memsahib had drawn a church she and Captain Keene might have attended. After that, there was an image of Abbu doing the dishes. I paused briefly, taking in the details of his kind, wrinkled face before turning the page. There was a drawing of a little pankha-walla like Vinay holding a fan half the size of his body.

And then there was a page with a drawing of me climbing the coconut tree in Vinay's mother's sari. I stared hard at the English words above my picture, but they just looked like swirls and lines. I didn't know what they said, and no matter how long I focused on them, I still couldn't figure it out.

But then I noticed Memsahib had drawn more coconut trees around me. And on each tree, there was a monkey gripping tightly to the tree in the same manner as me. The more I looked, the more I realized what Memsahib was saying. What she was comparing me to. What she really thought of me. Or rather, how little she thought of me.

A flush of embarrassment crawled over my skin. My shoulders began to shake as I covered my face and cried silent tears into my palms, trying not to be heard by anyone outside. How could she have written about me like this after everything I had done for her? Who else had seen her drawing of me? Who else *would* see it? Was this book going to be published in England like the other memsahibs' books the collector had mentioned?

My legs shook a little as I wiped my face. I had to get back to work. But how could I pretend everything was normal when I had been betrayed by my mother, betrayed by my father, and now betrayed by Memsahib?

With my pouch of wages swinging around my waist, I took Memsahib's rotten journal out of our quarters. I started for the bungalow, scraping past the tree outside. A branch scratched my shoulder blades hard. I gripped the journal harder and ran through the house, ignoring the pain. But it stung, just like looking at Memsahib's journal had—a sharp, unexpected jab to the back.

Chapter 26

I found Memsahib in the dining room, sipping a cup of chai as Vinay fanned her. The steam was curling around her face, making her hazy and unrecognizable, like she wasn't the person I had first seen. But maybe I just hadn't been able to recognize who she really was, since any small gesture of kindness from her had made me think of Ma.

Memsahib smiled at me. "Is that awful racket done outside?"

I nodded, and the breeze from Vinay's fan coiled the steam this way and that.

"The things these people will do," Memsashib muttered. "All because of some cartridges. Can you imagine? How utterly foolish."

Vinay's fan was moving back and forth, over and over, like it would never stop. I might not have been a rebel, but even I understood the sepoy mutiny last year was about much more than cartridges being soaked in the fat of animals whose consumption was against two religions. It was about fighting back, about stopping people who thought they were better than you from ruling over you and killing other Indians. It was about getting control back over your land and your destiny. It was about life and death.

And it wasn't utterly foolish. But like the fan, Memsahib kept going.

"Don't they get how much better off they are with us in charge? No one's hungry. Why, you even seem to have put a few pounds on your tiny frame since you started working here."

I thought about Bhavani's father starving to death, and my mouth went dry.

"Less violence," she said, turning so the fan cooled the back of her neck.

I swallowed, trying to heal my parched throat, trying to find my voice, as I remembered how the collector had flogged Chhaya, as I thought about Javed's battered face.

Memsahib took a long sip. "No sati."

I cleared my throat and held the book out to her.

"You found it!" Memsahib stood up with a start to pat my head, and, taken aback, I dropped the journal.

"Sorry," I said. I forced a smile as I bent down to pick up the journal. It had fallen on its face, its covers wide open like a bird.

As I turned it over to close it, though, I realized what page it had fallen onto. I froze, staring at the image I never wanted to see again. My eyes stung. My throat felt tight.

Memsahib's face turned pale, and Vinay looked down at his feet, obviously trying not to get involved. "That's just a drawing," Memsahib said, clenching the button on her blouse. "It was a silly joke." She snatched up the book, almost knocking her head into mine, and snapped the pages shut. "I was trying to be as witty as the collector's wife, I suppose. I— Oh, why am I explaining myself to you? You're just a . . . a . . ."

I watched Memsahib's gaze dart left and right as she searched for the Hindi word.

" . . . a child," she finished, standing up. She motioned for Vinay to follow her. Then she swaggered out of the room, head held high, holding the diary and trailing spiraling steam behind.

As the coils of steam dissipated and my vision cleared, I couldn't help but think what Memsahib had actually been trying to say was "just an Indian."

Chapter 27

I spent the afternoon churning cream into butter, cooking chickpeas, grinding roasted cumin into a brown powder, and slicing okra, potatoes, cabbage, carrots, and onions for the vegetable dishes I was making for Captain Keene's big dinner tonight.

A couple hours later, I stepped out onto the veranda to check if the yogurt had set from the warm milk and cultures I had left overnight in a covered bowl. I lifted the plate off the bowl and saw that wobbly, creamy yogurt had indeed formed. Just as I re-covered and picked it up, I heard a faint jingling. It sounded like my silver anklets, the ones that were bound up in my indigo pouch.

It was Lal, up in the gulmohar tree, the little bell still attached to his foot by a string.

I put down the bowl and whistled at him. My arms out, I tried to coax him my way with a wave of the hand. "Lal! Come here."

The bird cocked his head and looked at me with his red eyes. In that instant, it felt like he and I were the same being, and I could feel how much he loved his newfound freedom, how light his soul felt, how natural this was for him.

He blinked, and just like that, the moment was over. Lal flew off, his bell announcing his liberty to the world.

With Lal gone, the lightness I had briefly experienced disappeared. Instead, I felt tired. Tired of the sadness. Tired of the resentment. Tired of the lies. Tired of living whatever life those in charge told me to live, be it Babuji or the captain. Most of all, I was tired of pretending everything was okay. Because none of this was.

Javed was most probably being hanged right now on makeshift gallows by the magazine in front of the townspeople, his life over. Chhaya had a permanent twisting scar across her shoulder blade, like a gnarled tree root, from where the collector had hit her. Bhavani had seen her father starve to death. Abbu was giving up what little time he had left to serve the Keenes. Vinay's sole purpose in life was to make sure another person wasn't too hot. And I was taking orders from a woman who didn't even see me as human.

As I picked the bowl of yogurt back up, I watched Bhavani pluck cilantro in the garden across from the gulmohar and wondered what it would be like to taste true freedom like Lal—to not have anyone ordering me around. After all, wasn't life under the Keenes, no matter how comfortable it was, the same as life under my father? And how life with Krishna and his in-laws would have been? And was any of this any different than what millions of Indians were forced to do under the rule of people who didn't consider us their equals? Who thought of themselves as the best humans and us as just beasts of burden to order around?

What about making my own rules? What if I didn't just follow anymore? Maybe I was wrong not to have cared about the rebels' cause. Maybe it should have been my cause too.

"Meera," Memsahib said from the hallway.

I turned, spotting her through the barred wall of windows around the veranda door.

For the slightest second, she looked down, the way I did when being ordered around to show respect to the person ordering me. But then she straightened herself and lifted her chin, like she was reminding herself she had nothing to be embarrassed about, that she had done nothing wrong. "Tell Dharamveer to bring me my dinner in the sitting room tonight while the captain dines with his friends." Then she walked into the study and closed the doors.

I felt as unsteady as the yogurt, wiggling in its dish from my movements, as I took a hesitant step back into the house to do as I was commanded.

❧ ❧ ❧

At dinner, I stood with Dharamveer and Salim in the dining room. Before us, the long wooden table was covered in the feast we had cooked. There were a couple dishes of mutton biryani and chicken that Abbu had made. Next to them was a dish of chickpeas simmering in a tamarind sauce; two platters of vegetables and fruits; a spread of different sabjis made out of okra, potatoes, and cabbage; a raita with cucumbers and the yogurt I had made. In the middle of the table were dozens and dozens of flatbreads. The rotis glistened

with ghee, and a stack of parathas stuffed with potatoes and spices had a cube of butter melting down it.

Captain Keene sat at the head of the table, a bead
of sweat trickling down one of his blonde sideburns
as Vinay fanned him. He said something in English to
the seven British men at the table, and they all laughed
and then began to eat. I didn't know what he said, but
recognized the English word for *rebel*.

A skinny British man with large pointed ears and
long sideburns, who I recognized as the man who'd hit
Javed earlier today in the procession, grinned and said
something back.

I turned to Vinay, but he shook his head ever so
slightly, like he was telling me he couldn't interpret in
front of everyone.

I sighed, picking up the empty water pitcher near
Captain Keene, and headed back to the kitchen, as the
captain said something else, and I picked up the words
rani and *Jhansi*.

In the kitchen, I crouched down by Abbu in
the corner. He had set aside three little helpings of the
vegetables, chickpeas, and roti on plates made of
banyan leaves for me, Vinay, and Bhavani, who would
eat on the veranda. I smiled gratefully at him and took

a bite of the okra I had made. It was good, sweet and tangy and savory and crunchy. It had a citrusy burst of lime in all the right places, a pop of pepper when you would least expect it. And it had just the perfect amount of namak. Ma would have been pleased too.

I bit my lip, tasting the salt on it, realizing I was feeling proud of what I had made, yet that food was going to feed people who didn't think the person who made it was worthy of anything but serving them.

Vinay walked in with another pitcher on a tray. "More water, didi," he said.

I poured water from the clay vessel into both pitchers on the tray and handed them to Vinay.

"What did the captain say when everyone laughed?" I asked.

He hesitated.

"What was it?"

"Captain Keene said the rebel is no longer a problem."

I squeezed my fingers in a fist. Javed was dead.

"And after you left the room, he said soon Rani Lakshmibai won't be a problem either. They got word she had to flee Jhansi. Sir Reese said he was surprised there were any rebels here, given that he had never met a people so eager to please, so ready to obey, than Indians. He said it is in our culture to obey." Vinay gave me a sympathetic smile as he headed back into the dining room to serve everyone water.

Obey. I suddenly felt like a street dog again, chewing my leftovers up like Munna. Despite the delicious okra, there was a bad taste in my mouth. I needed to talk to Bhavani. I needed to apologize.

As Vinay left with the water, Dharamveer entered the kitchen. I handed him the plate with Memsahib's food. Abbu was busy chopping up more carrots and cucumbers, so I headed out to the hall with a clay lamp and Bhavani's food.

Bhavani was visible on the veranda through the barred windows, patching some holes in the captain's shirt in the dim light of a lantern.

I could hear more of the hollow sounds of the East India Company men laughing on the other side of the bungalow. They were laughing at Javed's expense. At all of our expense. At what they had done to our land, our resources, our artisanry, our creations, our cultures, our religions.

I didn't only care about myself. I cared that this was happening. I had to try to help. If Ma had tried a little harder, she could have saved me. Maybe if I tried a little more, I could help save us.

Dharamveer closed the sitting room doors behind him, heading back to the dining room through the kitchen.

I didn't know if he would pass me again on his way to his next task. I didn't have a lot of time. I threw my braid over my shoulder and headed straight for the study, pushing the emerald doors open and closing them softly behind me. I set my lamp down on the desk. Bhavani had gone through the piles of papers on this desk several times. But had she opened the drawers? I wasn't sure she had ever gotten that far.

I pulled the top drawer out from the left side of the heavy desk. It made a grumbling noise, but with the company men so thrilled with Captain Keene torturing a rebel today, it wouldn't be heard by anyone. The drawer was full of documents in English. I rifled through them, but there was nothing that looked like a floor plan of the magazine or even a map. I pushed the drawer back in and opened the middle one.

There was a map of a town that didn't look like Indranagar, its edges all frayed. Below it was a map of a fort, but not the fort that the British had destroyed and turned into the magazine here. I lifted the pages up and looked at the next paper, shining the light from the clay lamp onto it.

My mouth dropped open. It was a sketch of the tiny remains of the sandstone fort. The magazine. It had images of sepoys outside and other markings on it in English. I pulled the paper out, being careful not to tear it, and folded it gently before sticking it into my blouse.

I pushed the drawer shut, grabbed the diya, and rushed out to the hall, softly closing the study doors. No one was in the hall or seemed to have heard me out there. I set the lamp down on the little stool by the veranda windows that once held Lal's birdcage and grabbed Bhavani's food. Then I threw the back doors open and rushed to her side, almost knocking the little lantern next to her over.

"You startled me!" she chided. "I almost poked myself with the needle. And you could have started a fire!"

I straightened my shoulders out and put Bhavani's food down in front of her.

"This was the emergency?"

I shook my head. "No. *This* was." I pulled the paper out of my blouse and unfolded it, and the angry wrinkles in Bhavani's forehead unfolded too when she saw what it was.

Chapter 28

"*I'm sorry,*" *I said* to Bhavani, as we headed through the town that night after cleaning up the dishes and food from dinner. We were on a mission to find Sepoy Charan and get him the paper I had found in the study.

Bhavani held up the hurricane lantern and guided us past the small homes and buildings. Groups of people were huddled around them, laughing, talking, eating all sorts of street food treats like paan, roasted peanuts, roasted gram seasoned with turmeric and salt, and puffy popped lotus seeds.

"I'm sorry too," Bhavani said, her free hand clenching the bottom of her blouse and the document hidden in it. "I wasn't a good friend to you. And I do want to hear all about your life too. What your ma was like. More about Ravi . . . I know you've been through a lot. I shouldn't have made all those comments about you not wanting to help the rebellion."

"I'm helping now," I said. "So no more thinking about the past. Let's look ahead to the future." I took the lantern from Bhavani so she could clench both her arms around the important paper.

"What about your money?" Bhavani asked. "And the future you were saving up for? The future home you were going to buy with that money?"

"What use is a home when your homeland isn't free?" I asked, blowing strands of hair out of my eyes. "Let's find Charan. I don't know if I'm as strong as you guys, or if I'm the right person for this fight, but I want to try."

Bhavani followed me past a couple of laborers sitting on the path. We were weaving our way through a crowd of people outside a sari merchant's shop lit up with lanterns when we collided right into a girl just a little taller than us.

"Watch it!" she shouted as we tried to help her to her feet. "Can't you see I'm pregnant?"

"Sorry," I mumbled, head down, eyes on my feet like I was in trouble with Captain Keene again.

I paused. I had to stop doing that. I could apologize while looking someone right in the eyes. I stood tall, head held high. And then my knees went weak.

It was Sheela. Again.

"Shurpanakha?" Sheela said, her eyes widening.

Bhavani used her right hand to pull my arm as her left held steady on her blouse to keep the paper in place. "Do you know her?"

In the light of the lanterns, Sheela's cheeks were rounder than normal. Her elephant bangles were tight on her wrist. Her belly was protruding. She was pregnant. She must have come home to her mother for her delivery, as was the tradition. She looked at me, her mouth agape.

"It *is* you!" Sheela grinned without a hint of kindness. She grabbed my wrist. "Just wait until the family hears about this." She started pulling me back down the path in the opposite direction of the barracks, away from Bhavani, who lost her grip on me. "Suno!" Sheela shouted into the crowd. I realized Krishna's older brother must be here with her.

It was all happening so fast, I was at a loss for words. After all these months, I'd been caught? I was going to end up punished by my in-laws for running? This couldn't be how it ended for me. It just wasn't right.

Sheela's sweaty fingers tightened on my wrist. I dug my heels into the dirt, causing her to almost fall again as Bhavani caught up with us.

"Just what do you think you're doing?" Sheela demanded.

"I'm not going with you," I replied, my voice high and nervous.

"You don't have a choice. You are Krishna's wife. It's too late for sati now, and you've brought dishonor to his name and your own parents'. But Krishna's parents and brother will deal with you now. Suno!" she shouted again into the crowd.

My eyes narrowed. "They don't *get* to deal with me. I'm not their property," I said louder, my voice steadying as I locked gazes with her. "And I'm not yours, either." I ripped her fingers off me. "Now go back home and pretend you never saw me. Come on, Bhavani!"

I sprinted back toward the barracks, feeling as brave as the rani of Jhansi.

"Don't you walk away from me!" huffed Sheela after me.

"I'm not walking. I'm running!" I retorted as Bhavani and I disappeared into the crowd. I ducked around sweaty arms and cotton clothes thick with the stench of hard work.

My heart was racing. There was no way Sheela would keep her mouth shut. Soon Krishna's whole family would hear that I was alive. And then Ma would hear too. And she'd know I was okay.

Bhavani smiled at me as we approached the barracks.

"What?" I asked.

She shook her head. "Nothing. Looks like the fighter in you is finally alive."

I hid my smile, feeling so proud of myself for standing up to Sheela. But I had to focus on why we were at the barracks. Sepoys were hurrying to and fro, lanterns in hands. Some were eating outside, leaning against the brick wall.

"Have you seen Sepoy Charan?" Bhavani asked. I swatted at a mosquito buzzing around my neck.

A sepoy with a thin mustache pointed toward four more sepoys sitting on the ground, drinking chai. We approached them, and I held the lantern up, illuminating their faces. But none of them was Charan.

"Have you seen Sepoy Charan?" Bhavani asked again.

The light flickered against a short man with a dimpled chin. "I'm Charan," he said, raising an eyebrow. "Who's asking?"

"Wrong Charan," Bhavani said, nodding at me to follow her as she walked away from the group.

"How will we find him in the dark?" I asked, running my thumb up and down the lantern handle. "This is hopeless."

"And I don't know anyone else who can help us," Bhavani whispered. "Didi didn't know the name of the man who gave her the journal back. Tejinder bhaiya has left for another town. Javed bhaiya is gone. It can't be safe to have this paper on us." She leaned against a tree, looking at the small patch of forest behind us. It was the same patch of forest that led to the abandoned bungalow on the top of the hill.

"I know the perfect hiding spot," I said, staring through the leaves.

Chapter 29

*B*havani and I hurried through the trees with our lantern, trying to find our way through the darkness to the brick wall that marked the start of Captain Keene's property. All around us, the owls hooted loudly. The crickets chirped. Snakes hissed, and bugs buzzed around our ears. But we kept going.

"We have to make sure Captain Keene doesn't catch us," I said, panting. "Make sure we don't leave any footprints in the dust on the porch."

"And make sure there really is no ghost on the hill," Bhavani added.

"What?" I shivered as some animal snarled in the distance and another yelped.

"I'm kidding—"

"Shh!" I said, hearing men's voices ahead. I huddled close to Bhavani.

We peered through the thicket, still nowhere near the brick wall. Eight men were huddling there by a tiny lantern, some in different kinds of turbans, some in topis, and one in a sepoy uniform.

It was Charan.

"What are you doing here?" Bhavani asked, rushing toward Charan as some of the men stood up, startled. "We've been looking all over for you."

"It's okay. They're with me," Charan said, looking between both groups like he was saying it to everyone. "They're not going to let the captain's show today stop us. They're not going to let Javed's death be in vain."

I nodded at Bhavani, and she dropped to the group's side, pulling the paper out from the bottom of her blouse. "Meera found a document. About the magazine."

Charan opened the paper up, skimming the words and images. He set it down, the flame of the lantern lighting up his eyes as he smiled.

"This shows the exact location of the cartridges. The cartridges soaked in pig and cow fat. We destroy the magazine tonight."

Chapter 30

A few hours later, Bhavani and I crouched behind one of the trees about twenty feet from the magazine and barracks, our lantern waiting in the patch of trees behind us. The streets were a lot quieter now, with everyone having eaten and the shops all closed. A brown pariah dog was scratching his ear near the magazine before opening his mouth in a high-pitched yawn and walking away.

Sepoy Charan exited the barracks with a lantern. He straightened out his red jacket and walked to the four sepoys standing guard in front of the magazine. He pointed toward the barracks and waved the sepoys forward. They didn't budge, but it didn't matter. The seven men Charan had met with in the woods suddenly lunged out of the darkness from both sides, covering their mouths and dragging all four sepoy guards away from the door.

Charan pushed the heavy magazine doors open and rushed inside with his lantern.

"He's done it," Bhavani whispered to me. "We should get to safety."

I nodded and was standing up in the dark when one of the restrained sepoys suddenly broke loose and shouted, "Help! The rebels! Tall Charan is with them!"

I clutched Bhavani's elbow. Several sepoys rushed out of the barracks and swarmed the rebels, who quickly released the sepoys and dispersed. A few of them ran toward the market. One ran past us, rounding the barracks.

Charan raced out of the magazine in the chaos and headed for the trees behind us, shouting to the few rebels behind him. "The cartridges are gone! They're missing! Run!"

He sprinted into the trees, not realizing we were still there. Bhavani and I ran after him. He was too fast, though, and disappeared into the woods.

Bhavani scooped up her lantern from behind the trees and blew the flame out.

"How can the cartridges be gone?" I asked, gasping for air as we sprinted through the dark forest. "Were they sent to help fight Rani Lakshmibai?"

"All I know is, right now we have to get away from here. We'll have to climb the wall," Bhavani said.

I looked back, spotting a lantern behind us. "They're catching up to us," I sputtered.

Bhavani raced to the right. Up ahead we saw a hurricane lantern on the mossy ground.

It was Charan. His leg was tangled up in a vine. He was frantically trying to pull his foot out of his boot. It was almost out—but the vine was choking his ankle, making it impossible to escape.

Behind us, I could hear screaming sepoys. "Forget about me and get back to your quarters before you're spotted," Charan whispered.

It would be easy to leave him behind and save ourselves. But I knew what it was like to be abandoned, and I wasn't going to do that to Charan. "We're not leaving you," I said. I reached into my indigo pouch and grabbed a gold bangle. Turning it sideways, I slashed at the fibrous vine until it snapped. Charan pulled his foot out and reached for his separated boot.

I reached for Charan's boot too, and something glistened in the lantern light.

It was a silver toe ring on his bare foot.

I stared at Charan in utter disbelief. The words fell out of my mouth: "You're . . . a woman?"

Chapter 31

"*No time for explanations,*" Charan said, shoving the boot on as he stood up and grabbed his lantern. "Come on! Before they see our light."

Bhavani and I followed Charan through the woods, zigzagging around towering trees and pushing our way through bushes and thickets full of pointy branches. We sweated, and swatted at buzzing insects, and jumped around scattering rodents, until we reached the wall of Captain Keene's property.

Charan went to give me a boost, but I stuck my foot in a notch in the bricks and got over the wall easily without any help. Bhavani was right behind me, and then Charan crawled over.

We crouched behind the wall and the cover of trees

near the bungalow on the hill, listening for the sepoys. The thought of the ghost on this hill wasn't that scary compared to being caught rebelling against the British. I huddled next to Bhavani, gripping her arm tight with sweaty palms. But the sepoys' voices got farther and farther away, until we didn't hear anything at all.

I let out my breath, and my shoulders relaxed.

Charan exhaled shakily. "Nobody knows. Nobody knows I'm a woman."

I couldn't believe it. I looked at Charan's long nose, kind eyes, and dimpled cheeks. Sepoy Charan wasn't just a brave soldier. Sepoy Charan was a woman. A woman strong enough to be a sepoy. A woman fighting against the East India Company.

"The British arrested my husband, a sepoy, for his part in the rebellion. He was imprisoned in Delhi, set to hang with the rest of the rebels. I didn't know what to do, but I knew I had to help him. So I cut off my hair," she whispered. "I put on his clothes and set off, desperate to find news of what had happened to him. To see him again. I wanted to be taken seriously, so I thought if I pretended to be a man and became a sepoy, people would respect what I said. That they would listen to me. And it worked."

"So you hurt people in Delhi to save your husband?" I asked, a little nervous that she might do the same to me to keep her secret.

Charan shook her head. "I didn't hurt anyone. I want the violence to stop. But I did use the chaos as an excuse to get to the prison." She began to massage the cuts around her ankle where the vine had scraped her. "When I got there, though, most of the prisoners had already escaped in the mutiny. I finally got to see my husband's face again." Charan flinched. "But he was gone. Trampled in the chaos." Her eyes glistened, but she blinked them dry.

She hadn't mentioned sati. That meant her family must have been in the majority of Indians who didn't practice it. "So why didn't you go home after you were widowed?" I asked.

"And do what there? I know I shouldn't be wearing these after being widowed," Charan said, running her finger across one of the silver toe rings. "But they remind me of my husband. They remind me of what I've lost. They remind me of what I have to do—get the British out. Because of them, my husband is dead. Because of them, Javed is dead. Because of those cartridges that they've hidden, hundreds and hundreds more will die next. Do you know what Captain Keene did an hour after Javed died? He and the other officials raised their glasses in a toast to the corpse of India. That's what this place is to them: a body to bleed dry until it's no longer of any use."

A tear plopped onto my hand. Charan was crying.

"I want to stop them. I want to have hope. But I'm running out of it. I'm beginning to think they're unstoppable, that this rebellion is pointless."

I watched her break down, shoulders shaking, and couldn't stop thinking about how brave she was. Charan wasn't a distant figure like Rani Lakshmibai. She was someone I knew, someone I looked up to, proving just how strong women could be. I couldn't see her losing hope, like the embers inside her were being stomped out.

"This isn't over," Bhavani said softly, apparently thinking the same thing.

I squeezed Charan's hand. "She's right. Give us some time. We're going to find out where they've moved the cartridges."

May 1858

Chapter 32

*W*eeks passed, and we still hadn't found any clue about the cartridges' whereabouts. Bhavani and I had passed the time telling each other more and more about our families and our opposite upbringings. Bhavani couldn't believe my father had hit my knuckles for wanting to learn. And I couldn't believe just how much she had learned when her father sent her to school. We kept discovering more about each other all while learning nothing more that could help our rebellion. We were stuck. And with the suffocating heat of May now all around us, making us feel even more trapped, I wasn't sure how Vinay managed to fan Captain Keene all day without crying from exhaustion. But somehow the little boy always did as he was told and never complained.

That afternoon, Captain Keene talked with other East India Company officials in the sitting room, staying cool thanks to Vinay's hard work. Memsahib, who was barely speaking to me these days, was up on the front balcony, probably sketching more terrible images to send to England.

Bhavani and I were on the front porch. My indigo pouch, now almost full of coins, flopped against my waist as we shook plates full of dry lentils, sorting the rocks out of them.

"The British are being even more careful after Charan got into the magazine," Bhavani muttered. "We're wasting our time here."

"I know," I said softly as I could so Memsahib wouldn't hear us above. "But what can we do? I've checked the study twice now. I haven't found a new map." I flicked a brown stone away from the green moong on the plate.

Bhavani whispered back, "What's the point of staying in this house if it isn't going to help us—"

Before she could finish, the collector hurried up the porch steps. I was so startled I knocked over the plate of lentils.

"Captain!" he shouted, entering the house as Bhavani and I hurried to pick up the scattered lentils.

It was no use, though, because two more horse-drawn buggies arrived with Sir Reese and other officials.

I took a few steps down the stairs as the men rushed onto the property. I glanced up at Memsahib, who was leaning over the balcony and chewing the end of her pencil with concern.

I dashed back to Bhavani as the men headed toward the porch. "Do you think they caught Charan?" I whispered.

Bhavani shook her head. "Can you try to see what's going on?"

I nodded, and we ran along the wraparound porch until it reached the veranda in the back.

"Take a rag!" Bhavani whispered to me as I opened the back door.

She was right. It was the perfect cover. I grabbed a rag from the kitchen and crouched on the hallway floor, scrubbing at the day's footprints while trying to listen in on the commotion behind the closed sitting room doors. But all I could hear was muffled English, including a few words I understood like *rebel* and the Hindi word *rani*.

I snuck a peek into the seam between the sitting room doors. The sunlight was pouring in, but if I moved my head just so, the glare was minimized, and I could see that the captain was pacing. Vinay was having a hard time keeping up with him to fan him. Lots of men were shouting.

Just then the doors rattled a bit, signaling they were about to open. I ducked back as sunlight streamed through the opened doors, barely avoiding a fan in the face, care of Vinay.

"What is it?" I whispered to him.

"They need water," he said, motioning to the kitchen.

We began pouring glass after glass of water in the kitchen for the captain and his guests, while Cook banged some dishes around, frantically trying to put something edible together for the sudden company.

"What happened?" I asked Vinay again softly.

Vinay set the glasses on a tray. "It's the rani of Jhansi. She's made it to another city."

I couldn't believe it. "Her army kept her safe?"

Vinay shook his head. "That's the thing," he said, heading toward the sitting room with the tray as I followed. "It's not just her men fighting the East India

Company. The rani is too. She's leading her men in battle." He ducked into the sitting room as the men's commotion grew louder.

I couldn't help but smile. The mere mention of a woman—that, too, an Indian woman—had brought a roomful of British East India Company men to their knees. It was like she was showing the world a girl could do anything. Even change history.

I rushed to the wall of windows in the back hallway, brushing a small fly away from my ear. Bhavani was waiting on the other side of the veranda.

"Well?" she whispered.

"Rani Lakshmibai has escaped and is fighting the British off!" I whispered back.

A huge smile crossed Bhavani's face.

"What are you two whispering about?" asked a voice behind me.

I turned. Memsahib stood by the study doors, blowing on her chai to cool it down.

"I . . . I was just telling Bhavani that there would be dishes to wash when Captain Keene's guests leave," I said, surprised by how quickly I was able to come up with a cover story.

Memsahib took a long sip of tea, never letting her

eyes off us. "I can't believe there's so much rebellion in this land after all we've done to help these poor people. Isn't it a shame?"

I snuck a glance at Bhavani through the corner of my eye, and then looked back at Memsahib. "I suppose so," I said softly, my toes clenching at the slate tiles beneath my feet.

"Well, I hope I can trust you to keep us safe. To warn us if you hear of trouble. We have been nothing but kind to you. To all of you." Memsahib turned her back and headed for the sitting room.

She could say all she wanted about kindness, but I knew the truth. I smiled as the sitting room doors opened and the powerful golden rays from the windows inside caressed me with warmth and hope.

June 1858

Chapter 33

I sat with Abbu, playing pachisi by the tree outside our quarters as Vinay watched. It was hot and muggy, almost like the June air was as tense as Bhavani and I were, waiting for the rains to be released the same way we were waiting for some information we could use to help the resistance. Waiting to figure out where the cartridges could have been moved. Waiting to find out where Charan was and if she was okay.

Bhavani had gone for her usual visit with her sister, hoping like she had for days now that some rebel would stop by the collector's house to give Chhaya an update. But I wasn't holding my breath for some answer to magically show up for us. There had to be something we just weren't seeing that could help.

"Do you think Rani Lakshmibai is going to defeat the British in Gwalior?" I asked, still wondering if the cartridges had been moved so many miles away to try to defeat her. "She's been fighting for so long."

"I've been around a long time," Abbu said. "I've found that there isn't much hope in the future if you keep wondering when or if the British will leave, instead of accepting that this is how it is." He coughed into his shoulder, fresh drops of blood joining the old stains on his sleeve, as I rolled the shells and let Vinay move a piece for me.

"There is hope, Abbu," I replied. "I've found you can sometimes stand up for your own future."

"Smart move," Abbu said, rolling the shells and moving a piece four spots over.

I wasn't sure if he was talking about what I said, or the game, or both. I rolled my shells and focused on the board, trying to figure out what my next move should be, when a raindrop fell on my hand.

I craned my neck up, like Abbu already was, smiling as I remembered how Ravi would run out squealing with glee, hands outstretched, when it rained during the monsoon.

As more and more rain fell, Abbu quickly bundled up the pachisi board. "Another day?" he asked.

I nodded, squinting through the raindrops. The water felt cool and refreshing, like it was washing some of our worries away. Too bad it couldn't really.

Vinay held his arms up to the sky and began cheering as he hopped in puddles. Most of the servants were outside, taking in the sight.

I ran through the rain to check if Bhavani was back, unable to stop myself from beaming at the invigorating downpour despite my worries. I made my way around the trees to the side gate and peered out.

Handfuls of people were laughing in the streets, enjoying the cool relief of the rain after so many weeks of high temperatures. Kids were jumping and splashing, their palms up to the sky like the rainwater was nectar from the heavens they could hold forever.

I was tired of standing with my palms out, just waiting for more information to fall into them. I had to go find it for myself. "Let me out, please," I said to the two guards standing outside the iron gate door and under the shade of a tree.

One of them left the protection of the tree's canopy, getting drenched as he opened the door for me. I ran to the left, along the brick wall that surrounded the Keenes' property. I turned right where the road met the wall and headed for the collector's house. Through the small groups of people on the street and the pelting rain that was now really coming down, I saw Bhavani standing in front of the collector's gate talking to Chhaya, who was wearing her red blouse and white sari with its gold border and holding a lantern. Next to Bhavani stood another woman in a sari identical to Chhaya's. A large pouch perched on the woman's hip, and her head was covered by the pallu of her sari, but it wasn't doing much to shelter her from the rain.

I sprinted to a stop next to them. "What's going on?" I huffed.

The woman turned toward me, and the pallu fell off her head. I gasped. She had shorter hair like a man's, but I recognized her gentle eyes. "Charan?"

She pulled the pallu back over her head, putting a finger to her lips as her dimples showed. "I explained everything to Chhaya," she said softly as the rain pummeled the banyan tree in the collector's yard. "The East India Company is looking for a sepoy rebel who entered the magazine, not a woman." She pointed to a cotton sari fashioned into a sack on her hip. "My uniform is in here, in case it comes in handy later, but we may not have a lot of time."

Chhaya nodded, glancing back at the bungalow behind her. "The collector's wife and the children are leaving for England. Memsahib said she doesn't want to take a chance with all the rebellions," she said, talking about her own memsahib. "She wants to leave with the children . . . and she wants me to go with her."

Bhavani's face fell. "What? But the rebellion has been going on for over a year. Why does she suddenly feel the need to leave and take you with her?"

Chhaya reached through the gate's iron bars and tucked one of Bhavani's wet locks of hair behind her ear. "I guess the attempt on the magazine made her realize this tiny little town isn't as safe from rebels as she thought it was. The collector told her the cartridges have been moved from the magazine and that the rebels would never find them, but she wouldn't listen. They're leaving in three days."

"So tell her you quit," Bhavani said.

"I'm going to. In two days," Chhaya said. "That means we have two more days to work on finding information at both of our houses so we can track down those cartridges. After that, it will just be up to the two of you."

Two days. We hadn't found anything out in a couple weeks now. How would anything change in two days? Despite how optimistic Rani Lakshmibai made me feel about the future, maybe Abbu was right about letting go of hope.

❧ ❧ ❧

I tossed and turned in my sleep that night. The rain had stopped, and the air didn't feel as heavy as it had earlier. But I was still weighed down by the possibility that our resistance was losing ground.

I sat up. Vinay, his hair still glistening from the rain, was fast asleep. So was Bhavani. I took a breath and stepped outside, wincing when something poked the sole of my foot. I bent down to pick it up.

It was a cowrie shell from our game of pachisi. I ran my finger down its little mouth, thinking about how proud I had felt when Abbu had said "smart move" to me during our game, and wondering what the right move would be in our rebellion with just two days to solve everything.

Then a faint noise caught my ear. I squeezed the

cowrie in my palm and took a few steps out. The wind carried more quiet noises from behind the servants' quarters.

I pinched the shell between my lips and climbed the tree in front of our doorway, pulling myself up the slick branches. My foot slipped, and I caught myself, gripping the branch tight. I paused for breath, hoping I didn't make too much sound, then climbed higher and higher, not giving up until I could see over our quarters through the patch of trees behind us.

Off in the distance, there was movement at the bungalow on top of the hill. Lights bobbed in front of the house we'd been warned to keep away from.

The light wasn't a ghost, though. It was people, holding lanterns. I could make out the faint shadow of an arm or leg every now and then when the lanterns moved just right.

I thought about that sprawling bungalow, standing there alone, abandoned with nothing of interest inside. I thought about the ghost stories that had spread like wildfire, engineered to make people avoid the place. I thought about how the bungalow looked like many other homes around here, ordinary, worthless. Like what Babuji thought of me.

And then I thought about how very wrong Babuji was.

I grabbed the cowrie shell from my lips and clenched it tightly in my fist. I knew what my next move was going to be.

Chapter 34

*I*t *had rained heavily* through the night and the next morning, and the earth was soaked. I stepped around earthworms in the damp soil as Bhavani and I walked through the market, searching for a bag of salt, and wheat to grind into flour, which Cook had sent us to get for dinner.

I craned my neck as we walked past some weavers in their cramped homes, weaving emerald green and indigo threads into gorgeous cloth on large upright wooden looms as shoppers passed. "Where is she?"

Bhavani shrugged, whispering, "Charan said she would find us in the market today if we needed her."

We came upon a group of women in saris, shirtless men, and kids, their ribs showing, hands out, begging for money. I reached into my indigo pouch, handing over some coins. One of the men raised his feeble arm with great effort and put his hand on our heads, blessing us.

Bhavani blinked quickly, her eyes shining.

"Thinking about your father?" I asked.

She nodded. We paused by the salt merchant and purchased a small bag with the coins Cook had given us. Bhavani held on to it as we moved down to the stall selling flour, where I bought a bag.

"How will Charan know we need her?" I asked, hoping I could change the subject and help Bhavani feel a little less sad.

"I'm not sure," she replied, scanning the people around us. "Hopefully she's here somewhere, watching us."

We pushed our way through the crowd, full of people who were probably trying to get their shopping done quickly before it rained again. The air was muggy, and my sandals sank into the soft soil with every step.

A woman in the crowd collided with me, and I almost lost the bag of flour. But the woman caught it right before it hit the ground.

Bending down to pick it up, I saw that the woman was Charan. I breathed a sigh of relief and smiled. She had found us. She had been watching for us.

"I think I know where they are," I said quickly, taking my time to lift the bag and collect myself, buying time to share information without raising suspicions if someone from the bungalow saw us talking to a strange woman. "The bungalow on the hill."

"I can't find anyone else," Charan said, standing up next to me and putting her hands together in a namaste to greet Bhavani. "They've scattered. It's just me."

"It's not just you. We're here too," Bhavani said as people brushed by us. "We'll meet you there tonight."

Charan nodded, pulling her pallu farther down her forehead, and disappeared into the crowd.

I felt the weight of the flour in my biceps. "Do you really think we can do this?" I asked Bhavani.

We stepped away from the noisy crowd and moved toward a group of laborers huddled around a fire on the damp ground, a coil of smoke rising from it. "We have to try. Look around us. People are desperate. People are suffering. People are starving." A faint jingling caused her to stop in her tracks.

I turned toward the sound.

"Meera, don't—" Bhavani warned.

But it was too late. I turned and saw the emaciated laborers were roasting a featherless dead bird. It wasn't a chicken. It was much smaller. Like a songbird. On the ground, just to the side of a pile of black feathers, a little bell was jingling away in the night, thanks to the breeze.

"No!" I sank to my knees, clutching the bag of flour even tighter.

It was Lal.

My Lal. My friend. My little bird, who had finally gotten a taste of freedom just to end up dead.

My arms went weak, and I started to sob loudly. I couldn't help it. Bhavani put her arms around me, but I was inconsolable. What was the point of Lal's life? Living all those years in a tiny cage where he could never spread his wings, then finally getting a taste of what it was like to be liberated, only to be killed? What had he done to deserve this ending? All he'd deserved was freedom.

"Stop looking at it, Meera," said Bhavani, taking the flour from my limp arms and pulling me away as I wailed harder.

My eyes began to swell from my tears as I got to my feet. What if I also ended up dead after daring to try for a taste of freedom? I crossed my arms, hugging myself, desperately wishing Ma were here to hold me, to run her fingers through my hair. To rock me on her lap and tell me everything was going to be okay.

Bhavani led me back toward the bungalows. "They're starving and saw an opportunity for food. I know it isn't what you want to hear, Meera, but they're only trying to survive."

As we turned down the path toward the Keenes' property, I took the flour bag back from Bhavani, who was clearly carrying way more than she could handle. "I miss my ma," I said softly. "I wish I had never left her."

Bhavani nodded. "And I miss my babuji. But you wouldn't be alive if you hadn't left your mother, Meera. Sometimes when life is really tough, all you can do is look forward."

I played with the end of my braid, remembering how I had said something similar to Abbu when we'd played pachisi.

We walked silently through the back gate. After we dropped off the supplies with Cook, I watched the birds flying around the Keenes' garden. More birds perched on the walls of the veranda. I blinked hard, thinking of Lal as I helped Bhavani pull clothes off the line. They weren't totally dry yet, but this was as dry as they were going to get in the humid weather with rain threatening. I sniffled, struggling to pull Memsahib's heavy dress off the line with a long wooden stick.

I had to stop crying. I had to be brave like the rani of Jhansi, who was defending Gwalior from the British. I had to focus on the plan tonight. We only had two more days until Chhaya quit and we lost one of the only houses we had access to. I had to do this. I had to show the world—and myself—that girls could be useful. That we didn't just need to end our lives on someone else's funeral pyre. That we were valuable in our own right.

After all, where would the mutiny be if the rani of Jhansi had been forced to commit sati when her husband, the king, died?

I got the dress off the line, but it slid off the stick and fell on my face just as a huge whoop of celebration came from inside the house, followed by the sound of several men cheering. I pulled the dress off my head and put it in the basket, then raised an eyebrow at Bhavani.

When I rushed into the hall to see what was happening, Salim was exiting the sitting room doors, his head down and his lips scrunched up in sadness.

"What is it?" I asked, my hands rushing to my face like Salim's grief was contagious. "What are they celebrating?"

Salim's voice seemed to stick in his throat. "The rani of Jhansi . . . is dead."

My hands fell weakly to my sides. "What?"

"Captain Keene just received word that she died on the battlefield. They killed her. The British killed her. Rani Lakshmibai's rebellion is over."

On the veranda behind us, Bhavani's lower lip trembled like she was going to cry. Salim sniffled, wiping away his tears as he ducked into the kitchen.

"How could it happen?" Bhavani asked. "Maybe it isn't true."

I felt crushed, like I couldn't move, but somehow I made my way to the veranda, where I sank down.

Bhavani crouched next to me, crying. "If even a queen with all her resources can't succeed in defeating the British, how can we?" Her voice grew soft. "I bet they'll move the cartridges back now too." Tears spilled down her neck. "It's over."

A nauseating quiver made its way up my throat. This was a blow. It was a huge setback. But I somehow couldn't cry. Maybe I was out of tears. Maybe I had finally used them all up on Lal, on Ma, on my past.

In the distance, thirty feet away by the mango trees, I spotted Memsahib walking around the garden with her journal and Dharamveer following her around. He held her stool, waiting to see where she wanted to sit.

Koels, sparrows, parrots, peacocks, and neelkanths chirped freely in the lush greenery behind them, which was even more vibrant than normal, thanks to the rains. Dharamveer walked respectfully behind Memsahib, turning left when she turned left, going straight when she went straight. He was following her lead, letting her control where he went, all so she could sell a book that told our story, that made fun of us, that said she and everyone else who was British were better than us.

I thought about what Ma had said, about being strong like fire, about having the strength to accept difficult things. That might be true sometimes, but it hadn't been true when I'd nearly been forced to commit sati. And it wasn't true now. I was going to show Ma and the world what strength really was. I was going to be strong like fire, and fierce like the flames of rebellion, growing, spreading, raging, blazing—all the things I wished Ma had been for me that awful night when I ran away.

"It's not over," I said to Bhavani. "We can't let the rani's fire die out. Don't forget what you told me just now when we saw Lal." My lips trembled as I remembered the awful sight of the dead bird. "You can't control the past. You can't change it. We can't change the fact that Lal is dead or that Rani Lakshmibai is dead, either. All we can do is change our future by taking charge of what happens next."

I stood up with the laundry stick, scooping up shirt after shirt after shirt off the line and dropping them into the basket. A koel's birdsong filled the air as I exhaled. My eyes met Bhavani's. "And what happens next is that we're going to stop the East India Company."

Chapter 35

The kite with the bird on it fluttered in the night sky as a gray mist hovered over the moon. We were standing in front of our quarters, close enough that we could hear Prasad and a few other servants chatting outside. Bhavani held a lantern up, but the sky was so thick with dark, billowing monsoon storm clouds that we could just barely make out the white kite. But the string pulling in my hand and the rolling reel in Bhavani's assured us it was flying freely.

"Chhaya's going to stay with the baby until it's time to go, right?" I asked in a hushed voice.

Bhavani nodded. "No one will be suspicious that way. We've got this."

"Whoever heard of flying kites at night?" Prasad

yelled after us, taking a puff of the beedi in his hands. "I told them the first day I saw you two that you weren't very smart."

I smiled at Bhavani as we ran to the trees behind the quarters. If only Prasad knew just how smart our plan was.

As we reached the tree line, we pulled the kite down and quietly ran around the thicket until we reached the base of the grassy hill. Captain Keene would not be happy to know we were back here. But Captain Keene was still toasting his friends over the rani's death at the bungalow, unaware of what we were about to do. We paused where the heavy foliage ended.

Charan stepped out from behind the trees to our left, back in her sepoy uniform.

"What are you doing in those clothes?" I asked. "They're looking out for Sepoy Charan. I thought you'd be safer in a sari."

Charan shook her head. "I have a plan. After you distract them."

We could see lanterns at the top of the hill by the old bungalow.

"They only have two sepoys guarding it," Charan added. "Probably to not raise suspicion. Or maybe because they don't know how many of us they can trust."

"The bungalow is small enough that we can find the cartridges quickly without a map," I said, my heart thumping in my throat. "But what if I'm wrong, and the cartridges aren't inside?" I wished I could stop sounding so unsure and unconfident.

Bhavani hugged the kite close. "There's something important up there, that's for sure. Don't doubt yourself. I believe in you," she said, sounding a lot like Abbu.

"Okay." Charan put her hands on our shoulders. "You distract, and I go in. Ready to do this?"

"Like Rani Lakshmibai," I replied.

Bhavani and I ran forward, and she released the kite, sending it into the air as thunder rumbled. I tugged at the string. "If it rains, the kite will be too soaked to fly."

"Then hurry!" she shouted as we sprinted faster up the hill, purposely giggling and creating a scene.

"Stop!" shouted one of the two sepoys from the darkness. He raised his lantern at us, and I could see his thick eyebrows that seemed to converge as one. "Just what do you think you're doing here? This is Captain Keene's property!"

I started reeling the kite back in, knowing we had to

keep the sepoys busy long enough for Charan to get to the bungalow without being spotted. "Sorry, sir. Please forgive us," I said, like I was standing submissively in front of Memsahib. Only inside, I was standing tall, because I had nothing to apologize for. "We work for him. We didn't know. We were just flying our kite."

"In the dark?" the sepoy snapped. The key hanging off his waist briefly shone in the lantern light.

"It's the only time we get to play," Bhavani replied, making her voice shake like she might cry.

The other sepoy spoke up in a gravelly voice. "They're just foolish little girls. Not rebels. What harm could they do?"

The other sepoy shook his head as the kite landed. "Orders are orders. No one can pass."

Lightning cracked in the sky behind them, catching the sepoys' attention and briefly illuminating the bungalow just as Charan, in her white pants and red coat, headed up the porch.

The sepoys ran forward. "Stop!"

And we ran right behind them, dragging the kite on the short line on the grass as we raced to help our friend.

Charan tugged at the doors, but they were locked.

"What's going on?" the bushy-browed sepoy shouted, rushing up the porch stairs. "How did you know to find us here? No other sepoys know!"

Charan kept her face down, but the sepoy pushed her shoulder, shoving her back a few steps. "I'm talking to you."

The gravel-voiced officer gasped, raising a lantern. "Sepoy Charan? Is that you?" He lunged for her, grabbing her by the arm.

"Wait! I have something to tell you!" Charan yelled, struggling to raise her foot to her hand.

I gasped, realizing what Charan was about to do. "No!" I shouted, dropping the reel next to the kite.

"Nothing you say will save you from jail. Or worse," said the mustached sepoy. "Accept your fate like a man."

"Why accept anything like a man?" Charan asked, pawing at the sepoys until she grabbed something off them and finally managed to kick off her boot. "See, I'm not a man." The silver toe ring sparkled in the light of the lantern.

The men stood there with their mouths agape, as if they were inviting all the mosquitos and gnats of the night to fly in.

"You're . . . a woman?" exclaimed the scar-chinned guard.

"A fearless woman," Charan said through her teeth, throwing something onto the porch.

"Now!" Bhavani hissed to me.

With the sepoys' attention totally on Charan, I ripped some paper off the kite like we had planned, and we ran up the porch of the ghostly bungalow. Bhavani handed me the lantern and ran her fingers along the wooden planks. She picked up what Charan had thrown. It was a key she had gotten off the sepoys in the scuffle. Bhavani stuck it in the lock on the doors, turned it, and yanked the doors open.

We ran in, bolting the doors behind us as the smell of old sandalwood furniture swirled all around. There, in the hall and spilling into the room in the back, were dozens and dozens of boxes. Bhavani pulled one of the lids off. It was the cartridges.

The cartridges we had been trying to find for months.

The cartridges that would be used to continue to colonize us and others. Cartridges that would make sure everyone here was always under British control. That guaranteed we would never have true freedom and a real say in our future. That would always lead us to the same future full of oppression, bloodshed, violence, and death.

I had had enough of all of it. That wasn't a future I wanted any part of.

A few shouts sounded right outside the house. The sepoys must have realized we had entered the bungalow. The front doors rattled.

"It's now or never," I said to Bhavani.

"Do it," she whispered. The front doors were now being kicked by the sepoys outside, the wood splintering. "Hurry!"

I steadied my shaking hands and poured oil over as many boxes as I could without dousing the flame.

A thunderous kick, and the bungalow doors burst open, revealing the sepoys. Charan was restrained by the bigger man, who held her arms back.

"Stop, girl!" shouted the guard with the bushy eyebrows.

I gritted my teeth and took a defiant step forward to yet another crate, letting the last drops of oil plop out of the lantern onto it. I wasn't the timid little girl who'd peed in her father's lap at the sight of fire all those years ago. I wasn't the terrified girl who'd run for her life last year. And I *definitely* wasn't the lost little girl looking for her place in the world a few months ago.

I was a growing blaze, and no one was going to stop me.

I opened the lantern's door and dipped the torn piece of the paper kite into the flame, setting it alight. Then, as the sepoys watched with open-mouthed horror, I dropped the paper to the oil-soaked wooden boxes.

The fire spread to the first box of cartridges.

No colonizers would ever use them against Indians.

"No!" the gravel-voiced sepoy shouted as he looked around frantically for something to put the fire out with.

"Fire!" I screamed, grabbing Bhavani's hand.

There was a whoosh as the flames spread, rising up the bungalow walls, making the air sweltering.

The sepoys stood frozen, blocking the exit as the flames crackled and spit sparks.

"Out of the way!" Bhavani shouted, shoving them.

"We have to get out of here!" Charan yelled to the guards. "You know what happened in Delhi when the magazine caught fire. Right now, before it explodes!"

The sepoys didn't take more than a split second to decide they didn't need to risk their lives for the British

East India Company anymore. They let go of Charan and scurried out the doors.

Charan grabbed Bhavani's and my hands and led us out. She released us, pausing to scoop up her stray boot off the front lawn as we all raced down the hill. "Get Chhaya and catch your boat before the oarsman leaves," Charan said, out of breath.

"*Our* boat," I huffed.

Charan looked at me. "Tejinder sent word to me. He's a few towns over. The resistance needs help."

"But—"

Charan came to a stop, and so did we, gasping for air. "You're going to be fine. And so am I. But my work's not done." She bent down to hug us both, her eyes shiny. "I think I'm going to need this more than you this time," she added, holding her lantern up as she sprinted toward the brick wall to get to the woods.

"Charan!" I shouted, my voice cracking as she scaled the wall.

She turned, taking one last look at us, the corner of her mouth curling up into a smile like it had all those months back when she'd first given me her lantern. I smiled back, grateful and sad, knowing I'd probably never see her again, and then Charan jumped out of sight.

"We don't have long before something explodes in there," Bhavani said. "And we need to get on the boat. We asked him to wait until we came, but who knows if he actually will?"

"I have to get Vinay," I said. "We can't leave him." I wished we had told him earlier, but there was no way to trust Captain Keene wouldn't have tricked him into revealing our plans.

"I'll meet you at the river." Bhavani ran to the right, heading for the side gate to get to the collector's bungalow, as I headed for the Keenes' bungalow. My heart drummed. My palms felt as hot as the fire. But I had to keep running.

I rushed into the garden and up the veranda, then swung open the back doors before barreling into the bungalow. I threw the study doors open, not caring who heard them bang against the wall, and startled at Memsahib's open journal. She'd sketched Bhavani and me on the veranda, hanging laundry, our heads down, subservient.

I slammed the journal shut, my chin up, and rushed out to the hallway, where I heard chuckling coming from the sitting room.

Its doors were now open, as Dharamveer walked

out with a tray of empty plates. Vinay was inside, right beside the captain and Memsahib. Fanning away.

I scrambled into the room, almost knocking over a strange horse head statue on a side table. A dozen men stopped their conversations to stare me down.

I took a moment to collect myself. To stop feeling the weight of the stares. To not feel like I was some strange creature in my own land. I straightened up. "Fire . . ." I said.

"What's that?" asked the captain, seated on a plush red chair.

"There's a fire! The bungalow on the hill is on fire!" I shouted, finding my voice.

The captain rose, his face a ghostly white. He ran past me to the hall and out onto the veranda, where he paused, staring at the blaze on the hill in the distance.

Memsahib brushed past me as she went after her husband.

"Water!" Captain Keene shouted back to the bungalow full of men. "Get to the well! All hands on deck! We need water!"

As the men hurried out, almost knocking me over, Vinay dropped the fan to get water. I followed him as he ran toward the kitchen to where Abbu was staring through the barred hallway windows at the fire in the distance.

Abbu ran back to the kitchen with us. He picked up a huge clay vessel filled to the brim with water, and some of it splashed out as I put my hand on his arm. He turned to me, coughing a little into his shoulder.

I shook my head, and Abbu's eyes scrunched up in disbelief. "Meera, did you have something to do with this?" he asked, setting the water down.

I bent down by his side and gave his wrinkled arm a little squeeze, hoping he could understand my answer.

Abbu's mouth dropped open, but before he could say anything else, I spoke up.

"You've served them for far too long," I said as Salim and Dharamveer and a handful of others ran past me, either to help with the fire or to abandon the Keenes. One of them accidentally stepped on my bare foot.

I was wincing at the pain when suddenly a massive explosion shook the earth, rippling down from the hill in waves. The powder in the cartridges must have burst. Vinay looked out the kitchen window as I ran with Abbu to the hallway windows and open door leading to the veranda.

In the distance, the bungalow was nothing but raging flames of orange, yellow, and red as the fire devoured it.

Memsahib stood on the veranda, frozen in horror as she took in the sight.

"You need to go, Abbu," I whispered. "To Fatima. Now. She deserves that. You deserve that. You can come with us. Please?"

Abbu just stood there, clenching the collar of his kurta, reshaping the drops of blood from his cough on the shoulder. Like a cut that would never form a scab.

Before I could say anything else, Memsahib rushed to the window. "Meera," she said shakily, extending a hand through the bars, "you warned us. I knew you would. I was just telling the captain how loyal and obedient you were. I knew you were a good girl."

She came through the doorway and held her hand out to me again. "Stay with me. You'll be safe here."

It was the most caring thing Memsahib had said to me in months, since before I'd seen her drawing of me, of the animal she had compared me to in her journal.

But it didn't matter.

I turned my back on her and gave Abbu's arm one more squeeze, my eyes filling with tears as I whispered one last desperate time to him. "Come with us, please."

I trailed off as Memsahib came inside, her eyes once again fixed on the blaze outside the windows.

"I didn't think I'd live to see Fatima again. But I didn't think I'd live to see the day this would happen, either," Abbu said softly, tilting his head toward the distant fire with a twinkle in his eye. "You've given this old man hope that anything is possible. But I'll slow you down, and you need to go." He nodded urgently in Memsahib's direction. "You don't need me to look after you anymore. You've got it handled." He smiled through his tears. "Go. Lead the way."

I squeezed Abbu's hand again, a lump in my throat. Vinay jogged past us, water pitchers in his arms.

"Meera," Memsahib said by the veranda doorway, her hand now shaking more than her voice as she turned away from the fire to reach her hand out to me again. "Meera, hurry."

I took one look at Memsahib and held my head high, feeling great relief in knowing it was the last time I would ever hear her give me an order. Then I brushed past her, following Vinay out the door.

"Meera!" Memsahib screamed.

But I didn't turn back. I raced after Vinay, who was running through the garden for the crowded well. Dozens of British men were ahead of us, along with sepoy units converging on the back of the Keene property now, water containers in hand. In the distance, the house was a ball of fire, stray columns and skeletal fragments of the walls peeking through the flames. Thick clouds of smoke were starting to coil out of it, like a venomous snake.

From the line of trees ahead, the captain glanced back at the chaos and spotted Vinay. "Come on, Vinay! Up here, lad!"

Vinay nodded and started to sprint forward to the mass of men heading up the hill. I raced after him, clenching his hand and pulling him to the side.

"What are you doing, didi?" he cried. "The bungalow is burning down! They will lose all their cartridges."

"How did you know they were there?" I screamed over the noise of people shouting at one another to figure out how to put the fire out.

Vinay shrugged. "I heard the officials talking to Captain Keene tonight before you came back. They said they had moved the cartridges there to keep them safe from rebels."

"They're all gone in the explosion. It's a good thing," I said, kneeling down by his side. "They would have used them on Indians like you and me. Would you have wanted that?"

Vinay looked down at the pitcher he'd been carrying. Water had spilled out of it onto his arms. "I don't think so."

"Of course you wouldn't have," I said, rising to my feet.

Vinay's conflicted eyes filled with tears. "But we have to put the fire out before it spreads!"

I shook my head and pulled him to the side gate, now swung totally open as sepoys and other East India Company men rushed onto the property. Charan and Abbu might not be able to come, but I could make sure that Vinay was safe with us. "That fire is destroying the cartridges that the East India Company wants to use on us. If they want them saved, they should be the ones fighting the fire. Not you. Not me. We deserve a new life. A better life. So will you come with me?"

Vinay paused.

"There isn't much time," I said over the din. "Will you join us? You'll never have to fan anyone again."

A small smile crossed his face at the thought. "My arms *are* sore."

"I know," I said, taking his tiny hand more gently this time, feeling its warmth travel up my arm to my heart as we exited Captain Keene's wall. "Come on. Let's go find our new home."

Chapter 36

While it seemed like most of the town was running up the crooked lane toward the bungalow on the hill, either to gawk or to help out, Vinay and I were the lone people heading downstream. We made our way through the crowd and the chaos, hearing the screams of horror. We passed the starving road builders, whose faces said what I was thinking: *That's what they deserve.* We rushed through the market, not stopping until the air filled with the smell of fish as we got to the banks of the river.

But Bhavani and her sister weren't there.

I glimpsed around. Our boat wasn't there.

There weren't any other boats on the water this late at night that I could even convince to give us a ride, either. And the fishermen and fisherwomen seemed to all have gone to see the fire.

Had Bhavani and Chhaya gotten stuck somewhere? Or had they decided not to join us?

Or worse, taken a boat without us?

In the distance, the bungalow was nothing but raging flames of orange, yellow, and red as the fire devoured it. Smoke wafted down the hill toward where the crowd was stopped above the market. It had the faint scent of sandalwood—like the smell the night I had run from Krishna's funeral pyre. But this time, the perfumed mist of gray wasn't sickening.

This time, it smelled like freedom.

Through the fog of traveling smoke, two figures rushed toward us. "Bhavani!" I shouted. Waving, Bhavani and Chhaya joined us on the shore.

"What are we going to do?" Chhaya asked. "Where are we going?"

"We're going to find more people to help," Bhavani said.

"We're going to spread our resistance like a wildfire," I said as a neelkanth flew by. I looked at Vinay. "And we're going to go to school."

The oarsman we had made arrangements with

finally drifted toward us in his little boat. He caught sight of the spectacle on the distant hill and couldn't look away.

"We're here for our ride," I called out to him.

The oarsman snapped out of his trance. Adjusting his turban, he eyed our motley crew up and down. "Do you have the money?"

"Of course we do," Bhavani snapped.

He steered his boat toward us.

Bhavani felt the sides of the skirt of her sari. "Mine's gone," she said, hushed but panicked. "It must have fallen off in the chaos."

Chhaya shook her head. "The collector's wife started asking me all these questions, accusing me of having something to do with the fire. I got so scared I left everything and ran when you came. This is all I could grab," she said, handing the oarsman a handkerchief with a few coins bundled inside.

"This will take you a couple feet down the river," he grumbled.

My throat felt tight. We had to get out of Indranagar before we got caught. I reached for my indigo pouch and handed the coins to the oarsman. "How far will this get us?"

"Meera!" Bhavani whispered. "All of them?"

"It's okay," I said. And it was. I wasn't using the money to buy property or land, but I was using it to get a fresh start in life, just like Bhavani had said. Besides, I still had the jewelry from my dowry.

The oarsman counted my money. He shook his head as a few drops of rain fell.

"We had a deal," I said, my arms weak with nerves, like we really were going to get caught.

"Circumstances changed," the oarsman replied. "You didn't tell me we'd be fleeing in the middle of a riot."

I hurriedly pulled the silver toe rings and anklets out of the pouch and handed them over.

"There are four of you," he said.

I grabbed my two wedding bangles out of the pouch next, putting the gold jewelry in the oarsman's beat-up hands. He looked at them, then at the burning bungalow as the rain began to pour down on us. "I bet the British will give me far more than this for turning you in."

"Who says we have anything to do with that fire?" Bhavani snapped.

"You just did." He smirked as the rain came down faster.

I wasn't sure how much the rain would help douse the bungalow fire. We didn't have time to find out. I reached into the almost-empty pouch and pulled out my mangalsutra. With my wedding sari, anklets, toe rings, and bangles gone, my mangalsutra was the last thing I had from home. The last thing I had to remind me of my earlier life. Of the marriage I'd had no say in. Of the life that someone else had decided for me. Of my future that was supposed to have been cut short.

Rainwater trickling down my face, I dropped the mangalsutra into the oarsman's cracked palm. "Do we have a deal?"

The oarsman smiled, stepping back on the tiny boat to make space for us to get on. "Where to?"

"Somewhere far from here," I said, giving Vinay's hand a squeeze as we boarded.

The boat began to go with the waves, heading down the river, away from my village, from Babuji and Ma. Away from Indranagar. In the distance, the bungalow was still burning away on its pyre. It got smaller and smaller in the distance, the flames just a flicker of harmless orange on the horizon, silence replacing the panicked screams.

We were going away, free. Free from the past. Free from the captain. But not yet free from British rule.

Bhavani bit her nails on one hand while holding tightly to Chhaya's arm with her other. Vinay was anxiously squeezing the edge of the boat, digging his fingers into the wood.

But I just smiled at the rippling river ahead. Its water was gently swaying, rocking us forward. Every now and then a rough wave would splash us with foam as it attempted to knock our boat over. But it failed every time.

I lifted my head high as the cool splashes from the river turned into mist. I didn't know what my future had in store for me. But I was going to survive, with or without a husband. Because I wasn't someone's property. I wasn't a beast of burden. And I wasn't a pet.

I was a girl.

Not a queen or a poet.

Just a girl named Meera.

And I was strong.

Author's Note

Strong as Fire, Fierce as Flame is the fictional account of one girl's experiences during a volatile period of injustice, racism, sexism, and deep unrest in history. I hope readers understand the gravity of the situation and know that no actions with fire or dangerous materials should ever be taken without adult supervision.

While this story, its characters, and the North Indian villages and town it takes place in are fictional, several of the concepts and incidents mentioned are based on historical events. But with so few middle grade historical novels set in South Asia in publication today, it is sometimes easy to assume everything in this book was the standard for everyone there in 1857. In reality, that is far from the truth, as the South Asian region is full of diverse cultures, religions, languages, and traditions.

The diverse stories and experiences that took place

in the South Asian region during the time of European colonialism have often been overlooked in books published years ago that many readers still treasure today as classics.

I remember being shocked in elementary school when I read *The Secret Garden* and recognized that part of the story took place in India. Growing up, I had never read a book that wasn't from India that had Indian characters in it. I immediately felt a deep sense of pride and a connection to the book. But as I read more, I couldn't shake this uncomfortable feeling that the book did not think highly of Indian people. They were in the background. The story was Mary's even when it took place in India. Indians were described as "not people" but "servants who must salaam to you." I was overcome with a feeling of embarrassment and deep shame. Books like *The Secret Garden* and work by Rudyard Kipling, like *The Jungle Book*, are just a few examples of how racist many "classics" from this time period can be. Native people are viewed through a colonial gaze. Their lands serve as exotic, thrilling backdrops to stories, but their people are rarely even treated like people. Their stories are in the background, unseen, forgotten, not important enough to be told on the page, while the colonizers' stories are prioritized.

When the inherent racism in these stories is pointed out, the idea is sometimes met with pushback. Excuses are made, saying it doesn't matter if someone finds something racist in these stories, because these books were written a long time ago, and that's just the way people thought back then. But that isn't the way *everyone* thought back then. That excuse is once again only thinking about the people colonizing, not the people whose lives were forever changed from being colonized.

I was inspired, in part, to write *Strong as Fire, Fierce as Flame* to challenge these notions. I wanted to tell the stories that weren't considered important, because they *are* important, and they shouldn't be hidden or overlooked. I peppered this book with several real-life incidents I found in my research to paint a more accurate portrait of what was going on in lands and nations where colonial powers had taken over.

The journals and diaries the British memsahibs write in this story are based on real journals and travel books. I based Memsahib's observation of the British dancing in the Taj Mahal on an excerpt from Fanny Parkes's writing. She was a memsahib who spoke fluent Hindi and described British ladies and gentlemen having a band play on the marble terrace of the Taj Mahal, as they danced "quadrilles in front of the tomb." Travel books written by memsahibs in India were widely read and passed around in the United Kingdom. They were one of the main ways people in the UK learned about the European experience in South Asia. These books were many times filled with derogatory, racist observations, including the animal[1] Memsahib compares Meera to. They used words like *indolent*, *cunning*, *devious*, *scum*, and *servile* to describe the South Asian population whose land they had invaded. They pointed out problems in the land they were in without acknowledging their colonial interference was also a problem. And they viewed the traditions, cultures, and religions of South Asia through a prejudiced, colonial gaze, in which the native ways were looked down upon, ridiculed, and considered backward or morally inferior.

According to author and historian William Darlymple, during the Victorian era, much of British colonial history was rewritten to take out the looting and plundering and reframe the brutality as an exchange of ideas, art, and railways from the West to the East.[2]

The toast Captain Keene gives "to the corpse of India" is one I borrowed from not a memsahib but the British governor-general of Bengal, Lord Wellesley, who said it in one of his toasts. The story the collector tells about buying an Indian baby for a few coins is also a true story from the early 1800s, as was the remark the collector makes, referring to Indian children as "swarms of little, naked bronze children," a quote which came from a magistrate stationed at Meerut.

---

1   Nupur Chaudhuri (1994) Memsahibs and their servants in nineteenth-century India[1], *Women's History Review, 3:4, 549–562, DOI: 10.1080/09612029400200071*
2   theguardian.com/world/2015/mar/04/
    east-india-company-original-corporate-raiders

I thought these true stories and quotes were necessary to accurately portray a colonizer's mindset, since many journals and books have been published glorifying colonialism.

In reality, colonialism was a vicious, cruel, racist practice that led to the deaths of millions of people around the world, and whose effects continue to be seen today.

I hope this book serves as a reminder of what the experience of colonialism was for those who were colonized. I hope this book tells just one small part of a much bigger story that has largely been erased in our lifetime. And I hope this book encourages readers to question who is being centered in colonial stories and in all stories, to find out who is telling the story, and to remember who is being left out. Because that *matters*.

Historical Note

Sati: Meera's experience with sati, the ancient but relatively infrequent tradition where a widow immolated herself on her husband's pyre, was not the norm for the majority of South Asian girls in the 1800s. But Meera's lack of opportunity due to her gender is something she had in common with many girls in South Asia in the 1800s, and is something she has in common with children all over the world, even today.

Sati was a fringe tradition carried out by a few families in India in the past. Some widows went willingly, seeing it as a sign of their virtue, and as a way to follow their husbands into the afterlife, or to purify their husband's sins through their virtuous act. Others were forced to. When the British collected statistics on sati in the Bengal, Madras, and Bombay Presidencies from 1815 through 1824, the total number of reported incidents was 6,632.[3] Sati was opposed in the 1800s by both Indian activists, like Raja Ram Mohan Roy, and British men, including Lord William Bentinck.[4] In modern-day India, sati is against the law.

Dowry: Dowry is land, wealth, or gifts given from the bride's family to the groom's. Examples of the practice of dowry can be found from many parts of the world, including Europe and Asia.

In 1661, a large portion of Mumbai, India, was actually given to the British as part of a dowry. When Prince Charles II married the Portuguese princess Catherine de Braganza, the "island of Bumbye" was part of her dowry. The prince then gave the island to the British East India Company, passing around a land and its people as if they were inanimate objects one could own.

Dowry is illegal in India, although some families do still practice it, despite it being against the law.

Child Marriage: Child marriage is still an issue in many countries. Worldwide, more than 700 million women alive today were married as children (before the age of eighteen).

---

3   Suttee Revisited: From the Iconography of Martyrdom to the Burkean Sublime by Monika Fludernik; *New Literary History* Vol. 30, No. 2, Cultural Inquiries (Spring, 1999), pp. 411-437.

4   timesofindia.indiatimes.com/home/sunday-times/Why-sati-is-still-a-burning-issue/articleshow/4897797.cms

According to UNICEF, more than one in three of these women was married before the age of fifteen. Child marriage affects boys and girls, but since girls are oftentimes married to older men, the issue of child marriage affects girls throughout the world at a much higher rate. A Save the Children report found that around the world, every seven seconds a girl under the age of fifteen is married. In the United States of America, the child marriage rates have dropped by half since 2000,[5] but five out of every thousand children ages fifteen to seventeen are married. In addition, at the time of this writing, two American states allow girls as young as twelve and thirteen and boys as young as fourteen to get married with parental and judicial permission.[6]

In India in the 1800s, many people began to oppose the practice of child marriage. One of them, Rukhmabai, refused to move into the house of her husband after she was married as a child, a couple decades after this story takes place. Rukhmabai wanted to go to school, but a married girl had to drop out of school unless she obtained her in-laws' permission to continue her education. Rukhmabai protested the marriage in court and went on to get the education she had fought for, becoming one of the first female doctors in India in the late 1800s.

5   pbs.org/wgbh/frontline/article/
    married-young-the-fight-over-child-marriage-in-america/
6   pewresearch.org/fact-tank/2016/11/01/
    child-marriage-is-rare-in-the-u-s-though-this-varies-by-state/

Schools for Girls: The school Bhavani attended is based on Bhide Wada, one of the first schools set up for girls in India. It was founded in 1848 by two women, Savitribai Phule and Fatima Begum. Although they faced a lot of protest and adversity, they succeeded in making the school a place to combat ignorance and "social slavery" for their female students. In the mid-1800s, girls often had to leave the few schools that existed for them after a couple years to get married.

Matrilineal Society: The matrilineal Indian society Bhavani mentions to Meera is in Travancore, in Kerala.[7] Married women there did not leave their home to go to their husband's when they got married, but instead, grooms moved into their bride's childhood homes. Women controlled the household, the way men did in other parts of South Asia. And the birth of baby girls was celebrated.

Board Games and Language: Pachisi, the game Meera plays with Abbu, is known in America as Parcheesi. Pachisi is just one of many games from South Asia that later became popular board games in the West, like chess, and snakes and ladders—also known as Chutes and Ladders. In addition, the word *thug* and many other words

---

7   caravanmagazine.in/vantage/what-end-kerala-matrilineal-society

like *bungalow*, *bazaar*, *jungle*, *bangle*, *veranda*, *loot*, *pajamas*, *khaki*, and *shampoo* came to the English language from South Asia.

Stepwells: Stepwells are large wells with a series of steps one can climb down to reach the water. These architectural marvels can look mazelike, depending on their size, and can be in several different shapes, including round or rectangular, and made up of several stories. Some stepwells have dozens of steps, and some have over a thousand. When the British came to India, they found the stepwells to be dirty and started using other types of wells. The last new stepwell was constructed in 1903.[8]

Rampur Greyhound: The collector's dog, the Rampur hound, is one of many endangered Indian dogs that are becoming harder to find because the British brought foreign dog breeds to India, which resulted in crossbreeding, and because of the preference for non-native dog breeds in modern-day India. Half of the indigenous dog breeds of India have died out and have not been seen in living memory.[9]

---

8 smithsonianmag.com/travel/review-vanishing-stepwells-india-180962637/
9 qz.com/india/971238/
   the-indian-dogs-that-are-dying-out-because-everyone-wants-a-labrador/

Swastik: The swastik, or swastika, Meera mentions is a symbol that dates back to ancient India. It is a symbol of well-being and good luck. It is also an auspicious symbol in other South Asian religions like Buddhism and Jainism and can be found in and outside of homes and in temples. The word *swastika* is a Sanskrit word, the ancient language of India. Hitler and the Nazis stole the swastika and tilted it at an angle to twist the ancient symbol into a symbol of hate and devastating cruelty.[10] The original symbol is still used in South Asia and by many in the South Asian diaspora today.

British East India Company and Colonization:

Colonization is the practice of settling in, taking control over indigenous people of a certain place, and imposing another belief system and government upon the existing culture. Centuries of colonization have led to huge shifts in the global economies of countries that were colonized, as many went from lands rich in resources to places that struggle, depleted of their wealth. Conversely, the countries doing the colonizing became wealthier as they stripped their colonized lands of their resources in order to benefit themselves. Colonization was a brutal practice in which religions and cultures of the colonizers were often seen as superior to the indigenous ones. The colonized people

---

10 timesofindia.indiatimes.com/bangalore-times/What-the-Swastika-means/
articleshow/994390.cms

were often treated poorly, with violence, and in many millions of instances, by losing their lives.

Countries that engaged in the practice of colonization around the world include Portugal, England/the United Kingdom, France, Spain, Germany, Italy, Denmark, Russia/the USSR, the Netherlands, Italy, Belgium, the Ottoman Empire/Turkey, and the United States.

Several European powers subjected the South Asian region to colonization, including the Dutch, Danish, French, Portuguese, and British.

Parts or all of the Indian subcontinent were known by several names at the time of this story, including "Bharat," and the Persian name "Hindustan." The region was not a unified nation-state but a land of many kingdoms and empires sometimes at peace, sometimes in the midst of lots of bloodshed. I chose to use the word *India* because the fictional villages and town the story takes place in are in modern-day India, but the region referred to by all these names include parts or all of the present-day nations of Pakistan, Bangladesh, Sri Lanka, and India, depending on who used these terms in the 1850s.

The British East India Company started off as a company that traded in silks and spices, but quickly evolved into a dangerous colonizer, an unregulated private company comprised of 250 clerks—backed by twenty thousand local Indian soldiers—that became the ruler of Bengal in the

1700s under the leadership of Robert Clive. The Company had no interest in making sure the region survived. They pillaged and stole from the subcontinent, torturing South Asians to find their treasuries and loot them. That wealth went to the West, primarily to the United Kingdom by way of the British East India company and later the British government. These brutal practices changed the South Asian region from one of the richest areas in the world to one of the poorest.

The British East India Company took advantage of the decline of the Mughal empire in India, the support of the British parliament, and the British East India Company's colossal army to take over many parts of South Asia, and by 1765 it had a monopoly on trade there. Economist Utsa Patnaik calculated that Britain took $45 trillion from India between 1765 to 1938. This is a conservative estimate and doesn't even include the massive debts Britain imposed on India in this period of time.[11]

The British East India Company was able to scam the South Asian subcontinent by taxing Indian goods through collectors and then using a portion of that same tax revenue to purchase the goods through traders. So, as academic Dr. Jason Hickel puts it, instead of paying for them out of pocket, the British "bought" the goods from weavers and

---

11 aljazeera.com/amp/indepth/opinion/britain-stole-45-trillion-india-181206124830851.html

artisans with money they had just taken from them. Some of the goods went to Britain and the rest were reexported elsewhere so the British East India Company could once again gain money, much more than they "bought" the stolen goods for.

In 1858, after the rebellion was over, the British Parliament transferred powers from the East India Company to the British government, also called the British Raj. The Raj allowed Indians to now export their goods directly to other countries, but those goods could only be purchased through Council Bills, which was special currency one could only buy through the British Crown, thus ensuring the money for these items went to England too. When Indians went to cash that special currency, they were given rupees out of the tax money that had just been collected from them. Once again, as Dr. Hickel says, "they were not in fact paid at all; they were defrauded."[12]

The cruel practice of colonization continued under the British Raj's rule for almost another century. The subcontinent finally gained its independence, and India was partitioned into the countries of India and Pakistan in 1947. (East Pakistan later became the country of Bangladesh.)

The Portuguese controlled the Indian territories of Dadra and Nagar Haveli, which didn't gain independence

---

12 aljazeera.com/amp/indepth/opinion/britain-stole-45-trillion-
    india-181206124830851.html

until 1961.[13] They also ruled over Daman, Diu, and the Indian state of Goa, in the middle of India on the western coast. Daman, Diu, and Goa continued to be under the rule of the Portuguese colonial forces long after 1947, finally gaining independence to join India in 1961.[14]

Puducherry, once known as Pondicherry under colonization, was under the rule of the French East India Company, and later the French government, until the 1960s, when it became part of India.[15]

The impact of colonization can still be felt in India, Pakistan, Bangladesh, Sri Lanka, and any country that was colonized, including the United States of America. Colonization sometimes separated populations into nation-states. Decades of colonial meddling has led to displaced people. And many countries have been left in poverty after colonial powers stole their riches and resources. Some colonized countries, like Haiti, even had to pay their colonizers "reparations" to get them to leave.[16]

The impact of colonization can also be seen in the countries of the European colonial powers that still retain the wealth that was moved to the West. And it is important to remember that the Industrial Revolution, which

---

13 britannica.com/place/Dadra-and-Nagar-Haveli

14 britannica.com/place/Goa/History

15 britannica.com/place/Puducherry-union-territory-India

16 forbes.com/sites/realspin/2017/12/06/in-1825-haiti-gained-independence-from-france-for-21-billion-its-time-for-france-to-pay-it-back

benefited these countries, didn't occur just through innovation. It came at a terrible cost to colonized people and lands, whose resources, riches, and lives were looted to make other people and lands prosper.

Famine: Although there was not a major famine in India from 1857 to 1858, when this story takes place, there *were* several devastating famines in India during the centuries of British East India Company and British rule, during which millions of Indians died. India once had one of the largest economies in the world and was one of the top five most powerful economic empires of all time.[17] As one of the richest regions in the world, India's textile and skilled artisan work was sought after worldwide. But during the British colonial involvement and rule, many Indians were forced to go into agriculture jobs, and most of the grain they grew was then shipped to England. When monsoons were weak and there was less rain than usual, farms didn't yield as much as they normally would, and the British still took most of the food. So locals who grew the food would starve, while millions of pounds of grain from India fed people in the United Kingdom.

With ten mass famines since the 1860s during the period of British colonization, an estimated fifteen million

---

17 fortune.com/2014/10/05/most-powerful-economic-empires-of-all-time/

Indians died due to these cruel practices. These famines and the exporting of grain continued into the 1900s, well after the events of this book ended. The devastating Bengal famine of 1943 killed three million Indians.[18] As with the famines of the 1800s, food was being shipped out of India to feed others. In this case, lauded British Prime Minister Winston Churchill, who had voiced his disdain for Indians—who he called "a beastly people with a beastly religion"[19]—ordered the diversion of food from India to "already well-supplied" British soldiers and stockpiles throughout Europe during World War II.[20]

Household Staff: The household staff of a large bungalow in India often consisted of the gardener (mali); the cook (khansama or bawarchi); a servant who washed the laundry (dhobi); one who cleaned out the toilets before there were sewers; one who dusted; a watchman (chaukidar); someone to handle the horses (ghodawalla); a bearer (baira) in charge of all the servants, and the bearer's assistant (khidmatgar), who would set the table in addition to helping the bearer; and the man or boy in charge of manually operating a fan (pankha-walla). Fans could be the kind Vinay uses in this

---

18 theguardian.com/world/2019/mar/29/
winston-churchill-policies-contributed-to-1943-bengal-famine-study

19 independent.co.uk/news/uk/politics/not-his-finest-hour-the-dark-side-of-
winston-churchill-2118317.html

20 content.time.com/time/magazine/article/0,9171,2031992,00.html

story or like a large panel of a curtain attached to a string that would be waved back and forth by a servant.

In 1857, servants did not eat food from the British households they worked for. Because Meera and Bhavani are children, and girls—who also would not have been employed at this point in history—I took the liberty of allowing the girls to eat from the captain's kitchen for the purposes of this story.

Barracks: The barracks built by destroying an old fort that Bhavani mentions are based on what really happened at the Red Fort in Delhi. Once the British seized the fort, they destroyed some of its existing architecture to build barracks, sacrificing the palace's beauty and culture so that they would easily have a preexisting wall around the barracks. In 1857 British government officials and soldiers destroyed parts of the Taj Mahal by chiseling precious stones and lapis lazuli out of the monument.[21] The stolen jewels Bhavani mentions are based on the colonial legacy of looting other countries of their native wealth, such as when the British took the massive Kohinoor diamond from the ten-year-old heir to the Punjab throne for Queen Victoria to wear.

Until 1725, India was the world's only source of diamonds. The world's oldest gemology texts came from

---

21 tajmahal.gov.in/history-of-the-taj-mahal.aspx

India.[22] The Kohinoor diamond remains part of the British crown jewels today, and can be seen on display in the Tower of London.

Juruoor Singh: The character of Charan is based on a real young woman in the early 1800s. She pretended to be a man by the name of Juruoor Singh and served as a sepoy for a couple years to try to save her brother, who was imprisoned for debt, by earning enough money to free him. When it was discovered that she was really female, she continued to serve and was treated with respect by her fellow sepoys. She was finally discharged and given a large sum of money, along with a recommendation to the nawab of the city where her brother was imprisoned, to place both siblings under his protection.[23]

Sepoys and the Sepoy Mutiny of 1857: The word *sepoy* is the anglicized version of the Hindi word for *soldier*: sipahi. Sepoys were native infantrymen in the East India Company's army in South Asia. The Sepoy Mutiny of 1857 is considered the impetus for the large-scale rebellion against the British that soon followed.

Although there were many underlying causes to

---

22 smithsonianmag.com/history/
true-story-koh-i-noor-diamondand-why-british-wont-give-it-back-180964660/

23 Broughton, Thomas Duer, *Letters Written in a Mahratta Camp During the Year 1809* (Archibald Constable and Company, 1813), 196–198.

the sepoy mutiny, it started in 1857 when the East India Company switched from their old rifle cartridges to ones that were greased. Rumors began to spread that the cartridges were greased with cow and pig fat. Because the sepoys had to bite off the ends of the cartridges to load their weapons, they were upset—eating beef is against Hinduism and eating pork is against Islam. Tensions began to rise further in spring when sepoys became convinced of the validity of another rumor, that the flour being sold in the markets was mixed with the powdered bones of bullocks.[24]

On March 29, 1857, a Hindu sepoy named Mangal Pandey, upset over having to bite into a cartridge greased with cow lard, incited others to rebel. They shot a couple of their commanding officers before Pandey was arrested. He was set to be executed for his actions on April 18, but, fearing a full-scale revolt, the East India Company moved his execution date up to April 8.[25] After Pandey's death, the rebellion continued to spread, with sepoys mutinying in various towns in April, until the big rebellion in Delhi in May.

The sepoys took the city of Delhi by surprise, attacking the British there. Some killed European women and children in the process. The sepoy siege of Delhi incited other Indian civilians to fight back against the colonial regime as

---

24 Malleson, G. B. *The Indian Mutiny of 1857* (Seeley, Service and Co. Limited, 1912), 62.

25 britannica.com/biography/Mangal-Pandey

well. During the chaos, the massive magazine where the British munitions were stored was blown up.

It took several months for the British to regain control of Delhi in September. And when they did put an end to rebellions, they often punished countless Indian civilians and Indian freedom fighters in cruel ways, including hanging them without trial or strapping them to canons to execute them.[26]

The Rebellion of the Rani of Jhansi: With the resistance now in full swing, mutinies were spreading across India. In Jhansi, the king died, leaving Rani Lakshmibai without an heir. According to Hindu law, the rani could adopt a son and name him as her heir, but the British did not recognize her adopted son as the legal heir and annexed her kingdom.

Some historians think that Rani Lakshmibai instigated the sepoy rebellion in Jhansi on June 6, 1857, in which many European citizens of Jhansi, including officers, clerks, and their families, were killed.[27] But there are several conflicting theories.

One such conflicting theory comes from Indian historian R.C. Majumdar, who wrote that the rani had nothing to do with the atrocities against the European citizens in

---

26 telegraph.co.uk/news/2018/04/05/
skull-indian-executed-cannon-mutiny-should-repatriated-innocent/

27 Majumdar, R.C. *The Sepoy Mutiny and Revolt of 1857* (Firma K. L. Mukhopadhyay, 1957), 270.

Jhansi and did not want to participate in a rebellion initially. But the sepoys mutinied and forced her to dig up her guns, or they would kill her.[28] Majumdar states that the mutineers forced her to pay them, and only then recognized her as the rani of Jhansi. The British initially believed that the rani was innocent in the murders, but later came to suspect her. She was unable to convince them of her innocence and only later, in 1858—when she realized she would be put on trial for the crimes she did not participate in—did she decide to fight the British.[29]

According to Majumdar, "once she arrived at this decision she never wavered for a moment, and fought with courage, determination, and skill, which won unstinted admiration, even from her enemies." This courage could be seen in March of 1858 when the rani's troops engaged in a fierce battle with the British East India Company at Jhansi. Even though they were surrounded, Rani Lakshmibai did not surrender. Instead, she and a handful of guards were able to escape and head east to join up with more rebels, where she took the fortress of Gwalior. She then went on to combat the British counterattack at Morar, where she fought on the battlefield dressed as a man and died.[30] Her

28 Majumdar, R.C. *The Sepoy Mutiny and Revolt of 1857* (Firma K. L. Mukhopadhyay, 1957), 276.

29 Majumdar, R.C. *The Sepoy Mutiny and Revolt of 1857* (Firma K. L. Mukhopadhyay, 1957), 298.

30 britannica.com/biography/Lakshmi-Bai

bravery inspired and continues to inspire countless Indians across the country.

The British East India Company, which had been in India since the 1700s, relinquished control of India to the British Crown in 1858. The violent uprising against the British continued for several decades on a smaller scale until finally, in the 1900s, led by Mahatma Gandhi and many others, a new era of the freedom movement began, that of nonviolent civil disobedience. India finally gained independence on August 15, 1947.

Several women were part of the freedom fight in the 1900s, including many who were imprisoned by the British for their involvement in the movement, and some who went on to serve as congresswomen. Nineteen years after India's independence, and a little over a century after this story takes place, a woman became prime minister of India in 1966.

While many societies have improved their treatment of girls and women, there is still a long way to go to achieving true equality in many countries, including the United States and India. This book is in honor of brave children everywhere, speaking up and speaking out against injustice, violence, patriarchy, and colonialism to ensure that equality and equity exists in their generation and beyond.

Timeline 1857—1858

- **March 1857** – The sepoy mutiny begins, led by Mangal Pandey in Barrackpore, who refuses to use the new cartridges rumored to be soaked in cow and pig fat.

- **April 1857** – Sepoys in Meerut refuse the new cartridges and are jailed. Mangal Pandey is executed for his rebellion.

- **May 1857** – Sepoys take Delhi back from the British. Emperor Bahadur Shah II resumes power there.

- **September 1857** – The Delhi siege ends with the British East India Company taking Delhi over again.

- **March 1858** – General Rose of the British East India Company surrounds Jhansi, and a battle begins. Rani Lakshmibai escapes along with rebel forces that arrive to assist her.

- **May 1858** – Rani Lakshmibai and the rebel forces flee to Kalpi. After a battle there against the British East India Company, which she and the rebel forces lose, they escape and take over Gwalior.

- **June 1858** – Rani Lakshmibai dies in battle at Morar, Gwalior against Captain Heneage and his forces.

- **August 1858** – The United Kingdom parliament passes the Government of India Act, transferring power from the British East India Company over to the British government.

- **November 1858** – The British government takes over direct rule of the subcontinent from the British East India Company.

Glossary

beedi: an Indian cigarette

beta: son or child

beti: daughter

bhaiya: title for an older brother

bhindi: okra

bullock: a type of cow

didi: title for an older sister

diya (*plural* diye): lamp

gadda (*plural* gadde): a mattress

ji: a respectful suffix added to a person's name. It can also be shorthand for "haan ji," a reverential form of "yes"

hasiya: a curved sickle blade attached to a wooden board

kurta: a tunic

laddu: a round-shaped Indian sweet

magazine: the area where gunpowder, cartridges, and canons were stored by the East India Company

mehendi: an orange-red dye made from crushed henna leaves. Mehendi is used to decorate feet and hands for weddings and has a cooling effect on the skin

memsahib: a respectful term for a European woman in India from the combination of the English word "ma'am" and the Hindi/Urdu word "sahib"

namak: salt

nawab: a ruler of a territory. The title comes from the Mughal era in India

paijama: pants worn with a tunic

puja: Hindu prayers

pyre: a heap of materials that can catch fire, used as part of a Hindu funeral rite to cremate a body

rangoli: a pattern or design made out of colored powder, lentils, grains, or flower petals used to decorate homes during holidays such as Diwali

rani: queen

roti: round Indian flatbread

sabji: a raw or cooked vegetable

sahib: a respectful title for a man

sepoy: infantryman in the British East India Company's army. An anglicized name for sipahi, the Hindi word for *soldier*

sati: a relatively infrequent ancient Hindu tradition followed by a small percentage of the population, whereby a widow would have to immolate herself on her husband's pyre

suno: a word to get someone's attention

swastik: an auspicious symbol for many ancient Indian religions, including Hinduism and Buddhism

talukdar: an aristocratic Indian landlord

thug: a Hindi/Urdu word meaning *thief* or *swindler.* It entered the English language in the 1800s, during British imperial rule

Acknowledgments

Strong as Fire, Fierce as Flame would not have been possible without the help of many friends, family members, and historians. I'm so grateful for their time and expertise.

A huge thank you to Dr. Madhav Deshpande, Dr. Toolika Gupta, Nalu Aaji, Anuja and Manjul Deo, Rashmi Upadhyay, and my parents for all the books, resources, and answers to my many historical and cultural questions. Thank you also, Aai and Dad, for double-checking my Hindi and reading several drafts of this book for accuracy. Any mistakes are mine alone.

Thanks to my amazing agent, Kathleen Rushall, for believing in this story when it was just a tiny seedling of an idea, and for helping it grow. I'm so lucky to be on this journey with you.

To Brynn, Anuja, Andrea, and Sarah Cannon for reading early drafts of this book.

Thank you to my editor and publisher, Stacy Whitman, for helping me grow as a writer and shaping this book into what it is today. I'm so proud to be able to tell Meera's story with you.

To cover illustrator, Kate Forrester, and designer, Sheila Smallwood, for the stunning book cover. To Sheila and Vikki Zhang, for the gorgeous map of Indranagar and for making that fictional town come to life. And thank you,

Elise McMullen-Ciotti, Hannah Ehrlich, Jalissa Corrie, Shveta Thakrar, and the entire team at Tu Books/Lee and Low Books.

Thank you to all my friends in the kidlit community, including the #2017MGdebuts, #TeamKRush, and the #RenegadesOfMG. To all the independent booksellers, bookstores, librarians, and educators who have put my books in the hands of so many readers. And to my readers for your letters and kind words; I'm so glad to be able to share stories with all of you.

Finally, thank you to Aai, Dad, Apoorva, Arjun, Leykh, Zuey, Sachit, and my family and friends for all your support, encouragement, and love.